The
Longest
Trench

Other Titles from this Author:

Writing as Geoffrey Lewis:
The Michael Baker Canal Trilogy:
A Boy Off The Bank	978-0-9545624-6-5
A Girl At The Tiller	978-0-9545624-7-2
The New Number One	978-0-9545624-8-9
Cattle & Sheep & Boats	978-0-9564536-3-1

The Jess Carter Canal Stories:
Jess Carter & The Oil Boat	978-0-9564536-1-7
Jess Carter & The Bolinder	978-0-9564536-2-4
Jess Carter & The Rodneys	978-0-909551-00-8

Other Canal Stories:
Starlight	978-0-9545624-5-8

The D.I. David Russell Crime Novels:
Cycle	978-0-9545624-3-4
Flashback	978-0-9545624-0-3
Strangers	978-0-9545624-1-0
Winter's Tale	978-0-9545624-2-7
Gameboy	978-0-9564536-5-5

Writing as S G Miles:
Misty	978-1-909551-47-3
Remember Me	978-1-909551-22-0
Slave Prince	978-1-909551-31-2
Thunderchild	978-1-909551-27-5
LightningMaster	978-1-909551-38-1

For more information please go to:
www.sgmpublishing.co.uk

The Longest Trench

Geoffrey Lewis

SGM
Publishing

About the Author:

Stephen Miles was born in Oxford, in 1947. Educated at the city's High School, and later at Hatfield Polytechnic (now a University), he pursued a varied career including periods as a research chemist, a professional photographer and a security guard.

After many years in the motor trade, he finally spent eight years as owner and captain of a passenger trip-boat on the Grand Union Canal. His writing began during this time, at first as a way of filling in the dark winter days when his seasonal business was in the doldrums. His first book, *Flashback,* was published in 2003, under his well-known pen-name of Geoffrey Lewis – he now has a total of seventeen novels and two collections of short stories in print, with many more planned in the coming years!

Remember Me was the first volume to include some of his short stories; *Misty* is a second foray into that field, the emphasis this time being upon stories with a supernatural twist. His other recent publications include a story set in Roman days and the first two parts of a fantasy trilogy; in this book he returns to his most popular genre of canal-set historical novels.

Amateur photographer, canal boater and American car enthusiast, he now lives in Kidlington, near Oxford where he enjoys a pint of 'proper' beer...

ISBN 978-1-909551-43-5

First Published in 2014 by:

SGM Publishing
Kidlington, Oxon OX5 2HW
info@sgmpublishing.co.uk
07792-497116

PREFACE TO THE ORIGINAL EDITION:

I met Harold Kain for the first time in the November of last year. I had been sent by my paper to interview him regarding his unfortunate accident, during his confinement in the Radcliffe Infirmary; many of you may have read my brief piece in the Oxford Sunday Telegraph of November 12th ult. Despite our hugely differing backgrounds, he and I immediately struck up a friendly relationship, and, as it was a Saturday afternoon and I had no other demands upon my time, I remained at his bedside in pleasant conversation even after I had acquired the information I required for the paper.

Harold has been a canal boatman all of his life. His manner and style of speech may seem rough and uncouth, but it quickly became clear to me that he is an intelligent man, and that although uneducated he holds, and is capable of expressing, firm and clear views upon many of the matters afflicting the world in which we all live today. He is a young man still, but his outlook upon life is of a conservative nature, perhaps arising from the long history of the canals, a form of transport some see as outmoded and being justifiably overtaken by the railways, and even by motor transport on the roads in these days of prosperity. He will argue, given the opportunity, long and hard for the continuance of the canals; and in his defence I will say that there still seems a viable place in our economy for their slow but reliable delivery of bulk cargoes. And he will readily confirm that he and his fellows find no difficulty in acquiring work, that the demands upon the working boatman now are as great as in earlier times.

But such is not my purpose in presenting this book. In the course of our first conversation I became fascinated with the manner and hazards of his life afloat, and we spoke of it at great length. As I have said, it was, by chance, the 11th day of November, the fourth anniversary of the ending of the Great War, and our conversation at last turned to the subject of the war and its effect upon his world. It was at this point that Harold became somewhat agitated, declaring that amidst all of the recognition given to not only the brave members of our armed forces, which he agreed was entirely justified, but to others such as the railwaymen, the not inconsiderable contribution of the boatmen to our glorious victory has been largely overlooked.

When I expressed not only my interest but my preparedness to listen to his opinions, he relaxed once again and proceeded to tell me a little of his own experiences during that long dark period of our recent history. I found his tale quite absorbing, but as time was now passing and I was expected home for my evening dinner I asked if I could return to speak with him further the following day, once my work was concluded; he agreed, and so it was that I saw him again, sitting at his bedside for some two hours the next night to the considerable annoyance of the ward sister. Still, his tale was unfinished, and I desired to know more, if not all that he could tell me; I struck an agreement with Sister Beatrice that I would be allowed to see him every evening during his continuing confinement therein as long as we did not disturb the other patients on the ward, as the idea was already forming in my mind to try to tell his story to a wider audience once I had learned of it all for myself.

And so it was that I returned to the Radcliffe on successive nights, to the perturbation of my family as well as the nursing staff, and began to take notes as Harold continued to speak to me of his life on 'the cut', as he refers to the canals, in the time of war. By the time he was finally released, to return to his work and his own family on the boat, I had enough material to begin to write his story in earnest. This book is the result, and if it goes some way towards redressing what he and his fellow boatmen see as the injustice of the lack of recognition for their wartime efforts, then it has achieved its aim.

I wanted Harold to know of what I had written before I published my text, and it was perhaps by more than blind chance that the opportunity presented itself this month, when his wife, whom I had met previously on the ward during his recovery, became confined with the birth of their first child. The women of the boats would normally give birth in their living cabins on

8

their boats, but hers had been a difficult pregnancy, and she was taken to the labour wards of the Radcliffe after being overtaken by a particularly painful labour as they returned to Oxford to load again at the gas works. Over the next two days, while she recovered from the birth, I was able to read out my text in full to Harold, who gave it his complete approval with merely a few very minor corrections, which I have now incorporated into this published version.

To conclude, it is my pleasure to inform you all that his wife, Ann, has given birth to a healthy baby boy, whom they have decided to name Luke. I hope that all of you who may read this story will join with me in congratulating them, and wishing them and all who live and work on the canals of the British Isles the very best of health and happiness, now and for the future.

Wilfred Stevens
Journalist, The Oxford Telegraph
July 1923.

PREFACE TO THE ANNIVERSARY EDITION:

I have been aware of Wilfred Stevens' book about Harold Kain's experiences during the First World War for many years. It never achieved the kind of circulation that he or Harold might have hoped for; in the 1920s, while England still celebrated the end of the war and the victory of the allied nations, there was little appetite for actual reminiscences of that time – the horrors of the trenches were something that people preferred to forget, and that revulsion rather spilt over onto other wartime stories.

I should explain that Wilfred was my mother's second cousin – we are an Oxford family, as many of my own readers will already know. "A bit of a relation", as the people of the boats would have explained such a distant relationship! With the present growing fascination with the history and times of that awful conflict, I picked the book up and read it again; and it seemed to me that it tells a story of those people, still largely forgotten even as they were when Harold complained to Wilfred from his sickbed, who worked the boats throughout the four years of the war, putting in long days through seven-day weeks in support of the war effort. Much of that work comprised the continuation of their peacetime work, but they also took on additional, and in some cases very hazardous loads that were directly related to the conflict – including ordnance in various forms, much of it highly explosive! Safer, no doubt, for it to travel by water than on the roads or railways.

Wilfred's writing is of its time – rather stilted to modern eyes, and perhaps not that appealing to today's readers. So I decided that I should rewrite it completely, making it (hopefully) more attractive in its style and vocabulary while not in any way detracting from the story that he tells. Much of the dialogue I have kept unchanged, but some I have 'modernised' a little and other parts I have fictionalised where there was no original dialogue and I felt it was needed to make the story flow. Wilfred's text clearly makes full use of Harold's amazing memory, a common attribute of the boating people as I have found myself in conversation with those I know – a people,

11

many of whom have never learnt to read or write, who depend entirely upon memory in the absence of written notes! And it would appear to me that, while Wilfred doesn't acknowledge it, parts of his story must have come from Harold's wife Ann, notably the story of her family and their own wartime exploits – this may have been told at second-hand by Harold, of course, again relying on that incredible memory.

I have added a lot of further research of my own, particularly into the various families, which has enabled me to flesh out the characters quite considerably, and my own knowledge of the canals and their ways and traditions has helped me to envisage many of the scenes that Wilfred describes and so add detail and, I hope, atmosphere to them. In rewriting his story, I have taken many liberties in order to make it more readable for a modern audience – but the essentials of it remain unchanged.

I have also changed the title: "A Memoir of the Canal in Time of War" is hardly likely to inspire a modern reader! "The Longest Trench" seemed to carry the immediate connection with what we now call the First World War, and perhaps to emphasise the boatmen's direct involvement with the conflict, albeit in a remote role - I don't intend to disparage in any way the sacrifices of those who served in the Flanders trenches, and I hope no-one will mistake my meaning in that way.

Be that as it may, I think this story is worthy of republishing at this time, with the centenary of the Great War, as Harold describes it, upon us. I hope you find it interesting, and if it finally does a little to bring about some recognition of the contribution of the boating people to the war effort, maybe it has finally achieved Harold's purpose!

Geoffrey Lewis
August 2014.

Chapter One

'Pa! PA!' Joseph Campling looked up from his shovel at the sound of his eldest daughter's voice. Their boat was tied in the basin at Oxford, half-empty now and beginning to bob about more as it rose in the water; their load, from the colliery at Newdigate near Bedworth, was destined for the brewery in Paradise Street. For now, they were unloading it onto the wharf-side into a stockpile from where it would be collected by horse-carts for the few hundred yards that would see its journey finished.

He turned another shovel-full of coal into the waiting barrow and paused, leaning on it as she rushed up to him:

'What is it Annie? Wha's all the h'excitement about?'

'Dad, there's a war on! They've just said so!' She stood looking down at him, her eyes alight, the bag of shopping clutched in both hands held in front of her.

'Ah, well, we knew as it moight be coomin' din't we? Never moind about it now gal, put yer shoppin' in the cabin and put the kettle on, eh?' He looked around: 'Coom on Beth, Jacob, Johnnie, we've got a job ter do!'

'Yes, Pa.' Annie looked deflated at his casual response to her news; she turned away and climbed down into the main cabin of the *Alice Rose* and stowed the various provisions she'd bought from the shops along Walton Street in the cupboards and drawers where they belonged; tins and veg in the table-cupboard, milk and meat in the cold-cupboard behind the coal-box, and so on. The stove wasn't lit in the warmth of the summer, so she put the primus on its flat iron top and set it going, pumping up the pressure, tipping a little methylated spirit into the cup and lighting it, opening the valve that would allow the paraffin vapour to escape and light in its turn. With the flame settled to her satisfaction, she took the kettle and stepped up into the tiny stern well of the boat, reaching around the chimney of the stove to tip fresh water from the decorated can in front of it into the kettle. Back down into the cabin, the kettle on the primus, she spooned tea into the big teapot standing ready on the table-cupboard's lowered door.

Outside, Joseph and his crew – his wife Beth, fifteen-year-old Jacob and eight-year-old Johnnie – had returned to their labours, shovelling the coal into large wooden wheel-barrows which they then wheeled up the planks laid into and across the boat, over the gunwale and onto the bank where the contents joined the growing pile earmarked for Morrell's. All were grimy and tired, but there was still the best part of seven or eight tons to go, and in the boatman's world time was money; the sooner they were empty, the sooner Joseph would be paid. And the sooner they finished the next trip, the sooner his next pay-day would come around! Their back-load was ready and waiting for them on the wharf – for Morrell's Brewery again, barrels of ale to be delivered to the basin in Banbury where drays would distribute them around the local public houses. Then it would be running empty to Newdigate again for more coal – it was a good regular contract, with loads both ways, and Joseph's income was more than adequate as a result despite the low rates paid on the canals in the face of railway competition. The whole trip would take them a week; he would aim to be at Newdigate ready to load on the Monday morning, Wednesday would see them unloading in Oxford, Friday delivering the beer to Banbury and so back to Newdigate for the next round.

In the cabin, Annie poured the tea, hot and strong. A splash of milk and two spoons of sugar into each mug, and she began to lift them two at a time onto the open slide above the cabin doors. The last one in her hand, a packet of biscuits in the other, she stepped up into the well again.

'Pa, Mam! Tea's oop, 'ave a break.' Like all boaters, she had developed the knack of raising her voice both in tone and volume so that it would carry for a considerable distance; faces all over the basin looked around, many of them with envious smiles. Joseph laid his shovel down on the remaining coal-heap with a sigh:

'H'okay Beth, boys – 'ave yerselves a rest, we ain't got too much more ter go.' They all stopped shovelling and gathered on the wharf beside the cabin, gratefully taking a mug and a biscuit from the packet as Annie tore it open and passed it around.

'What was that yeh said about a war, Annie?' her elder brother enquired.

'S'roight Jake! It were on the wireless in one o' the shops, an' they was all saying it's in the papers too. Seems loike soom fella, a duke or soomat, got 'imself shot in a place called Sarajevo. What that's got ter do wi' oos Oi don' know! But the war's on any'ow – they're callin' fer men ter go an' join the h'army.' Johnnie was gazing up at her with excitement dancing in his eyes, but Beth Campling turned to her husband with a worried look on her face:

'Oh Seph!' He slipped an arm around her shoulders:

'Don' worry Beth, it ain't goin' ter bother oos Oi don' suppose.' The world of international politics was far removed from their steady life, no more than a distant background to their labours, and to Joseph there seemed no reason for him or his family to have any part in them. Wars were fought in far-off lands by men who had chosen to serve in the army or the navy of their own free will, and to him that seemed the correct way of things.

'They're sayin' as this'un's goin' ter be a real big do though, Pa.' Annie spoke cautiously, afraid of disturbing his complacency. But he grinned at her, his equanimity unchanged:

'Well if there's a lot o' foightin' they'll need oos ter 'elp keep the beer flowin', won' they?'

'Yes Pa.' She smiled at him

'What else are they sayin', Annie?' Jacob asked.

'There'll be a lot o' foightin' fer sure, but they don' think it'll go on too long. They say as it'll be over by Christmas.'

'Oh well, there'll be no need fer oos ter trouble about it then' her father interjected. Jacob turned a thoughtful look on him, but he said nothing.

The tea drunk, the biscuits half-gone, they turned back to their labours. Annie quickly washed the mugs and stood them to dry on the cabin-top and then joined them, stepping in to push the loaded barrows out of the boat and empty them over the stockpile. It took them no longer than another hour to have the entire load out of the boat; twenty-three tons, all but, in half a day. Johnnie raised weary eyes in a coal-blackened face to his father with a cheeky grin; Joseph ruffled his hair as Jacob threw his shovel down and stretched his aching back. Beth climbed out onto the wharf-side and looked around:

'Them's ours over there are they, Seph?' She pointed to a row of barrels lined up at the back of the wharf. Looking up, he nodded:

'Ah. Johnnie, Annie, you sweep the bottoms out, sharpish, h'okay? We'll start rollin' 'em over.' The two youngest collected the shovels and stowed them in the front corner of the long narrow hold behind the fore-cabin, and picked up the brooms that stood there. They began sweeping energetically, side by side, moving the remaining coal dust towards the stern of the boat. Their father climbed out over the gunwale, and he and their older brother quickly took down the planks of the barrow-run – their own, which also served as the top-planks of the boat's running gear, they kept to hand, others, belonging to the canal company as operators of the wharves, they carried away to be stacked by the wall between the basin and Bulwarks Lane. That done, they walked over to the row of barrels and began to roll them, tipped onto their lower rims, over to the boat.

With the dirty part of the job finished, Beth took the mop from the roof of the cabin and set about washing down the paintwork of the cabin and stern, revealing in its full glory the bright colours and fancy decoration. Canal water sufficed for such things; satisfied with the result, she picked up the equally-brightly-painted water can from its place in front of the chimney and carried it over to a tap by the wall where she refilled it to the brim with drinking water ready for their journey back up the canal to Banbury. Its three gallons would be enough to see them there, and she could top it up again then before setting off up to the coalfields.

16

The hold cleaned, the sweepings shovelled out onto the bank, Annie and her little brother clambered out to leave the way clear for the barrels to be loaded, a job too heavy for them to get involved with. Beth went to join her husband and son; she and Joseph hefted the barrels between them, easing them up a plank relaid up to the gunwale and then over and down in to the hold where Jacob took part of the weight before rolling each into place, stacking them in compact fashion so that they would get the whole load fitted in. He filled the hold carefully, from both ends in turn, so that the boat settled evenly into the water; as it did so, the job became easier, the height of the gunwale coming down until at last they could dispense with the plank and tip the barrels directly over the wharf-edge into the boat.

Two hours later, the last barrel dropped into place. Joseph raised an arm and waved to his younger children – Annie and her brother had been fussing over Molly, grooming her, making sure she'd been fed and had plenty of water, refitting and adjusting her harness. The row of stables stood along the back wall of the basin; now they led the pony over to the boat, carefully going around the heaps of coal and stacks of boxes, cases and barrels that stood around waiting to be loaded into boats or delivered out into the city. They took her around the end of the wharf to the far side of the water where the towpath led back out of the basin around the bend and under the tightly-arched bridge to being their journey northwards; Joseph and Jacob quickly laid the top-planks in place, across the barrels rather than on the stands with this load, then untied the boat from its mooring and poled it across to the far bank. Jacob threw the towline, already attached to the top of the mast and laid on the fore-deck, to his sister; Annie hooked it onto the spreader behind Molly's hind legs and clicked her tongue:

'Go on Molly! Off we go!' The pony gave her a look over its shoulder that said 'I know what to do' and leant forward to take the strain of the heavy boat. It moved, almost imperceptibly; the rope slackened, Molly took a short pace forward and leaned again into the padded leather collar of her harness; the boat slowly gathered momentum and as it did so she began to walk forward, her pace increasing until they were travelling at a steady, easy speed. Under the bridge, Molly treading carefully on the narrow towpath under its close arch, and so out onto the Oxford Canal for the first stage of their trip. Annie stayed with the pony, walking at her heels; Johnnie, worn out after his exertions on the wharf, stepped over into the stern well of the boat where his father stood as it passed under the bridge, the heavy wooden tiller under his arm, guiding the boat along the channel but hardly seeming to look where he was going as he rolled a cigarette in his hands.

Chapter Two

As the *Alice Rose* had been slowly rising in the waters of the Oxford basin, two other brightly-painted boats had been doing the same, if rather more quickly, on the outskirts of Banbury. The *Avon* and the *Dee* were different from the usual kind of narrowboat, though – belonging to Thomas Clayton (Oldbury) Ltd, they were specially adapted to carry liquid cargoes. Their holds were covered by a wooden planked deck, curving slightly from side to side so that the rain (or shipped water!) would run off, below which the space was split into two enormous tanks accessed through hatches set in the decks.

The Kain family ran both boats – Alfred Kain, the patriarch, was the captain of both. A tall, broad-shouldered man whose sandy hair was greying with the passage of the years, he ran the *Dee* with Mary, his wife, and his only son Harold as crew; the *Avon* was entrusted to his daughters. Janet was nineteen, the eldest and in charge; Vera at seventeen was mate, aided by Susan and Emily, eleven and nine respectively. Their liquid cargoes, the tar residues from the manufacture of house gas, were easier to unload, pumped out of the holds with the aid of a steam-hose to liquefy them in cold weather; both boats were empty in short order, unlike the long and arduous task of shovelling coal.

Like Joseph Campling, Alfred had a regular job – Claytons held the contract to carry the tar produced at the Oxford gas works to Robinson Brothers tar distillery which stood by the canal just south of Banbury. He reckoned to get two trips in every week – the journey itself could be done in one long day, twenty-seven miles and fourteen locks, but depending upon what time of day they could set off he would usually make an overnight stop somewhere on the way. It wasn't a difficult schedule; they would often have the time to visit the new picture palace in Oxford, along Walton Street, and most weeks they would take a trip to the public baths in Banbury.

Mid-morning on that fateful Wednesday:

'Yeh ready ter go Jan?' Alfred called along the dockside to his daughter.

'Yeah, Dad, soon as yeh loike.' Her raised voice came back to him. He nodded brusquely and bent to untie the rope at the stern of the *Dee;* Harold stood on the fore-deck, the long shaft balanced in his hands; his mother waited on the towpath with Libby the mule, ready to take up the tow. Alfred and Harold poled the boat backwards the short distance to where the winding-hole, a widened part of the narrow canal channel, allowed them to turn it around; there, Harold drove the fore-end out across the water into the tip of the triangular cut-out in the bank. His father poled in the opposite direction, the stern swinging around, the rudder brushing the bank, until they were facing south again; Harold pushed the fore-end over until he could throw the towline to his mother. Snatching it out of the air, Mary dropped its spliced loop onto the hook of Libby's harness and gave her a gentle slap on the rump:

'Go on Libby, good girl!' The mule walked slowly forward until she felt the drag of the boat and then leant into the harness to get it moving; as it picked up speed and cleared the way, Janet and her sisters repeated the same procedure to get the *Avon* ready to follow. The two older girls wielded the shafts, their younger sisters waiting with their mule, Buddy; and then they too were on their way, following their father's boat a hundred yards or so behind.

They made good time through the brightness of the summer afternoon, ripening crops in most of the fields they passed between filling the air with their warm, dusty fragrance. Many of those farmer's fields were connected across the canal by bridges – wooden bridges that lay just above the water level and had to be tipped upwards out of the way to allow the boats through. It was Harold's job to run forward, lift each bridge and hold it clear while both boats passed beneath; then he would run forward again, either to catch the *Dee* or on some stretches to get to the next bridge in time to open the road for it, so close did those bridges lay to each other. Energetic work, but he enjoyed it, the freedom and exercise of being on the towpath instead of just sitting on the boat; and at each lock they passed through he would take pride in working the paddles and gates as quickly and efficiently as he could, even timing himself sometimes with the pocket-watch his parents had given him last Christmas.

The locks delayed their journey – but the narrow locks of the Oxford Canal fill and empty quite quickly, so that delay was a matter of minutes only. And the two crews worked together at each so their combined passage was smooth and easy all the way down the steady descent into the Thames Valley. Grant's Lock, King's Sutton Lock, Nell Bridge Lock, Aynho Weir Lock where the River Cherwell crosses the canal at water level, and so to the deepest lock of all – Somerton Deep, all twelve feet of it, the boats descending rapidly into a dark chasm as the water drained out through the open paddles. And so on and on – past Somerton village, past the Heyfords, Upper and Lower, the old canal twisting and turning its gentle way across the landscape; a swing to the west near Kirtlington, back to the east after Pigeon Lock, westwards again to Enslow where they passed under the railway for the first time.

At Baker's Lock their road became part of the River Cherwell, a length that could be treacherous when there was heavy rain raising the river into flood. Back into an artificial channel at Shipton Weir Lock; under the railway lines again, past Shipton-on-Cherwell and so to the right-angle bend and the heavy Aubrey's Lift Bridge in the village of Thrupp.

With dusk gathering, Alfred called a halt for the night. They tied the boats, breasting them together to allow space for others to moor at what was quite a popular stop; the youngest girls took the mules to the stables at the pub for the night, fussing over them, making sure they were fed and giving them a brisk rub-down. The crew had had their meals on the move – a pot of stew prepared by Mary, cooked slowly on the range in the *Dee's* cabin while potatoes baked in its oven, ladled out onto plates and passed from boat to boat, hurriedly eaten between locks or lift-bridges.

Thrupp's popularity among the boaters for an overnight stop arose from the village 'public' – the Boat Inn stood beside the towpath, along from the lift-bridge which in this case spanned the water to the Oxford Canal Company's maintenance yard.

After a quick wash and brush-up Alfred and Mary were ready for a drink before settling for the night:

'Can Oi come too Dad?' Harold had washed and brushed his hair in hopeful anticipation. Alf grinned at his wife:

'Shall we let 'im, love?'

'Don' tease the boy, Alf! After 'e's got 'imself all clean an' toidy.'

'Come on then boy!' At fourteen, Harold felt himself to be as good as grown up, not that the licensing laws would have agreed. But like most canalside pubs, the landlord at the Boat was happy to have youngsters around, even if he would keep an eye on what they were allowed to drink.

'Yeh comin', Jan?' Alf knocked on the side of the *Avon's* cabin as he emerged into the stern well of the *Dee*. His eldest climbed out of her cabin:

'Ready, Dad. Vera's goin' ter settle the girls an' then she'll join oos.'

The four of them stepped over onto the bank and walked the short distance to the pub. Outside it, a number of smaller children were playing together in the near-darkness; Mary gave them a disparaging look, feeling that they should all be in bed by that hour. Some were boatee kids, a few from the hamlet whose cottages stood along the side of the canal. Almost outside the pub they spotted a familiar face, a young girl sitting aloof of the younger children on the forecabin of her boat:

''Allo Annie! Yer Mam an'Dad insoide, are they?' She smiled at them:

'They're in the pub, mister Kain. Oi'm keepin' an eye on ar Johnnie; 'e's gorn ter bed.'

''Bout toime yeh joined 'im, ain't it Annie?' Mary suggested:

'Oi will soon, Missus Kain. But it's so noice ternoight, don' yeh think, just sittin' 'ere?'

'Aye it's a grand noight, girl! But don' you be too late ter bed eh?'

'Oi won', mister Kain.' She turned her smile on Harold: ''Allo, 'Arold.' Harold felt a flush creeping up his neck:

22

''Allo, Annie. 'Ow are yeh?'

'Oi'm foine, 'Arold. 'Ow 'bout you?'

'Oi'm h'okay thanks.' He stood looking at her, feeling slightly foolish. He'd known her and the Camplings for many years – travelling the same stretch of canal, all the boaters got to know each other. All were a part of that mobile, working community, almost a floating village; all were at least acquaintances, most were friends. But just as she'd spoken to him, he'd been looking at her with new eyes, thinking to himself what a pretty girl she was. Until that day, familiarity had made her just another kid he'd see from time to time, but sitting there, her dark hair shining under the one streetlamp, she'd suddenly looked older, and the sight had stirred something inside him.

'Yeh comin' in fer a drink, 'Arold?' His father's voice woke him from his reverie.

'Er – yeh, comin', Dad. G'noight then, Annie.' Her smile grew wider:

'Good noight, 'Arold.'

Chapter Three

Wednesday August the fifth, 1914:   The news of Britain's declaration of war had quickly spread through the boating community in spite of the inability of most of its members to read the newspapers.   In the bar of the Boat Inn, Alfred and Mary found Joseph Campling with his wife and son about to pay for their drinks:

'Alf! Mary, Jan – what will yeh 'ave?'

'Point o' moild fer me, an' a stout each fer the girls, if tha's h'okay Seph? An' a lemonade fer 'Arold?'   Frank Marston, the landlord, turned away to draw another pint and then opened two bottles, pouring them at the same time into two glasses; Joseph handed over a couple of coins and took his change:

'Cheers, Frank.'   He turned to Alfred: 'Ar Annie says there's a war on?'

'Yeah, s'roight Seph, we 'eard the same at Robinson's. Started yestidday, they said.'

'Wha's it all about then?   Annie said summat about some fella getting shot in – where was it Beth?'

'Sara-somewhere, weren't it?'

'Sarajevo.' Frank joined in from behind the bar.

'Where the 'Ell's that?' Alfred enquired.

'Bosnia-Herzegovina.'   Frank laughed at the stunned expressions all around him: 'It's a little country out in the east of Europe.'

'So what the 'Ell's it ter do wi' oos then?'   Frank leant forward, his elbows on the bar:

'Well, it's kind of complicated, Alf.   The fellow who got shot was the heir to the throne of Austria-Hungary, right? They've been having a go at Serbia, another country out there they want to take over, and the man who shot the Arch-Duke was a Serbian. So Austria declared war on Serbia. Russia didn't like the idea of Austria getting right up to their borders, so they came in on the side of Serbia, and that upset the Germans...'

'Complicated?   It's a bloody mad'ouse!'   Joseph interrupted, incredulous, getting nods from all around him. Frank laughed again:

'You're not wrong, Seph! Anyway, Germany's getting too big for her boots lately, you know?'

'Never loiked the look o' that Kaiser Bill fella o' their'n, stoock-oop sort o' bugger.'

'Arrogant sod, isn't he?   Anyway, they declared war on Russia.   But then they declared war on France too, afraid the French would take the opportunity to attack them from behind, and sent their troops into Belgium on the way to attack them first.   And we've got an agreement to support Belgium – so yesterday Asquith took us in on their side – which means we're at war with Germany.'

'Bloody 'Ell!   What a mess – what 'appens now then?' Frank shrugged:

'Not a lot, probably.   They'll fight it out amongst themselves – we're sending troops over to France to help stop the Germans, and the Navy's going to blockade the North Sea to stop them getting supplies.   They say it'll all be sorted out by Christmas.'

'Hnh. Shouldn' make any diff'rence ter oos then?'

'Can't see why it should, Alf.'

'Moight be some work in it, Alf? Gettin' stuff ter the docks fer the h'army, things loike that?' Joseph wondered; Alf shook his head:

'That'll all be down the Junction ter the docks in Lunnon, won' it?   There'll be nothin' down 'ere fer oos.'   Joseph shrugged:

'Well, we're h'okay as we are, ain't we?'

'Tha's roight Alf, we've got a noice steady run 'ere, ain't we?' Mary agreed.

'Aye, we 'ave, love. Let them others 'ave the war work eh? Oi don' fancy carryin' stuff wha's loikely ter go off bang any'ow!' A round of laughter greeted this, and the talk turned to other matters, things more relevant to life on the cut.

''Ow are yeh then, 'Arold?' Jacob asked as their parents settled to a discussion of the price of horse-feed. The two boys had been pals since childhood; as teenagers they were still as close as members of different crews could be.

'Doin' h'okay, Jake – 'ow 'bout you?' Jacob shrugged:

'Pretty good! You got beer on again then?'

'Yeah, ar usual trip. Ter Banb'ry wi' the barrels, then empt ter Noodigate fer coal. You goin' ter h'Oxford Gas Fact'ry?'

'Yeah, same as alwes. But it's grand ter be out this toime o' year, eh?'

'Yeah. Jake?'

'Yeah?'

'Um – 'ow old is yer Annie now?'

'Thirteen. Why yeh askin', 'Arold?'

'Oh – just wondered, tha's all. We saw 'er out there on ar way in.' Jacob raised an eyebrow, but he let Harold change the subject: 'Wha'd'yeh reckon ter this war then, Jake?' Jacob's brown eyes lit up:

'Sounds h'excoitin' ter me! Oi wish Oi was older, Oi'd go an' join oop.'

'Really?' Harold looked at him sceptically: 'Yeh wants ter go an' foight?'

'Why not? Be an adventure, wouldn' it?

'Yeah, mebbe...' Harold didn't sound convinced: 'We ain't old enough any'ow, Jake. Oi'll stick ter boatin', thank yeh!'

Susan and Emily Kain made their giggly way back from the stables; at the *Alice Rose* they paused to talk to Annie:

''Ello Annie! 'Ow are yeh?' She looked up from her reverie:

''Allo Suey, Emmie! We're h'okay. 'Ow's your folks?'

'We're grand! Lovely day, weren't it?'

'Oi love the summer!' Emily agreed with her older sister, and Annie laughed:

'Yeah, S'great ain't it? Yeh off ter h'Oxford agen?' The girls nodded:

'S'roight, ter the gas fact'ry.'

'Oi love goin' on the river! S'real fun.' Emily had the others laughing with her enthusiasm:

'S'long as the railway remembers ter send someone ter h'open that bridge! We've been stoock there fer ages sometimes.' Susan commented. The railway swingbridge over the Sheepwash Channel could be an obstruction to passing boats, taking time to open and close, and subject to the trains' schedules.

'Oh yeah!' Annie paused: ''Ow old is yer 'Arold now?' Susan frowned, surprised by the question:

''E's...' She added up quickly: ''E's fourteen, Oi reckon. Whoy?' Annie shrugged:

'Oh, just wondered. 'E's a nice boy, ain't 'e?' Emily stared at her:

'No! 'E's ar brother, 'E's a pest! Alwes tellin' oos what ter do.' Susan laughed:

'S'roight Emmie!'

'Well Oi think 'e's nice!' Annie disagreed; the two girls looked at each other:

_'Oh...'_

But before Emily could make any further comment they were haled from along the towpath:

'Coom on you two! 'Urry oop, yeh should be h'in bed by now!' Their sister stood with her hands on her hips waiting for them; Susan grinned at Annie:

'We gotta go! See yeh Annie!' They dashed off with a backward wave to her.

At the pair of Clayton boats, Vera quickly settled the two girls to bed, squeezed in top-and-tail on the side-bed in the _Avon's_ living cabin; brushing her hair, she left them there and stepped off to join her sister and the rest of the family in the nearby bar. Just in time for her father to be buying a round of drinks for his family and friends, she joined the comfortable, relaxed conversation. Talk had turned to family matters:

'Wha's yer brother on now, Seph?' Mary Kain had asked.

'Siah? 'E's subbin' fer Barlow's, same as oos. 'E's mos'ly on coal from Pooley ter Banb'ry Co-op – we sees 'im sometimes oop that end o' the h'Oxford cut. They're doin' h'okay, 'e reckons.'

''Ow's yer Mam copin'?' Alf enquired.

'H'okay, thanks. Bit of a shock fer 'er, Pa goin' sudden loike that. Was fer all of oos.'

'Yeah.' Mary's tone was sympathetic: ''Is 'eart, weren't it?' Joseph nodded:

'S'roight. Wen' out loike a loight, walkin' down Hythe Bridge Street. By the toime the h'ambulance got there 'e'd gone.'

'She still in the cottage, Seph?'

'Yeah, down Fisher's Row. 'E's buried in Jericho, at Saint Barnabus's.'

'Aye – sorry we weren' there, Seph, we'd 'ave loiked ter 'ave seen 'im off.'

'Yeh missed a good do, Alf! We went ter the Bookbinders an' 'ad a few fer 'im.'

''E got seen off in style then?'

'Oh ah!'

Their second round of drinks finished, the crews broke up and headed back to their boats. Alf and Mary Kain quickly settled into the cross-bed of the *Dee,* while Harold sat in the darkness in the stern well. He'd been vaguely disappointed, but not really surprised, that Annie had disappeared into her own bed by the time they left the pub; that brief sight and even briefer conversation had left him with the thought that he'd like to see her again. They would inevitably meet before long, but that would usually mean just a few snatched words as their boats passed, a 'hello-goodbye' called across the water but little else.

He heard the rustle from below as his mother pulled the curtain across which separated the two parts of the cabin, and stepped down inside himself after a last look around the still, silent night. His mattress was already in place on the narrow side-bed; he undressed and settled for sleep, pulling the rough blanket around his shoulders.

In the *Avon,* the two youngest girls were already sound asleep; Janet and Vera climbed down into the cabin as quietly as they could. Vera had dropped the flap and mattress of the cross-bed before she left for the pub, and they too settled for the night, Vera pulling the curtain across to give them a little privacy. Space on the beds of a narrowboat's cabin is always tight, but they like their parents had grown up with those conditions, squeezed onto a side-bed when they were small just as their younger sisters were now; as soon as he had felt they were old enough to handle the job, their father had asked his employers for another boat, so that now the whole family had more sleeping accommodation. And double the earning capacity, too.

The *Alice Rose* had been built for Joseph Campling on Sefton's boatyard at Tusses Bridge, near Coventry on the Oxford Canal; his older brother had inherited their father's old boat, the *Sarah Ann*. Both were owner-boatmen, known on the canals as 'Number Ones', their work either picked up independently or, as now, sub-contracted to one of the bigger carrying concerns. Now that his family was growing up, the previous year Joseph had taken the boat back to Seftons and had the tiny fore-cabin fitted. With Jacob now a teenager, and Annie getting older too, he'd taken the decision to lose a small part of his loading capacity rather than risk the wrath of the local health inspectors who had the duty of checking the boats for compliance with the law; a law that restricted the numbers and ages of children who could share their parents' accommodation.

That night, he and Beth sat in the well and smoked a last cigarette apiece; below, Annie was already curled up asleep on the side-bed. Jacob had disappeared into the fore-cabin he shared with little Johnnie; after a few minutes they too climbed down inside and were quickly abed. The morning would see an early start – up soon after daybreak, which meant around 5 o'clock on a summer day, and on their way by six. Late afternoon would see them unloading the barrels of beer onto Banbury Wharf; the next morning, after an overnight stop in the town, they would be heading back to Coventry and the coalfields.

Chapter Four

The next Tuesday afternoon: The *Alice Rose* was just south of Banbury, travelling at a good steady pace, on time to reach Oxford with its twenty-two tons of coal the following morning. Molly was trudging her usual cheerful, uncomplaining way along the rather ragged towpath, Johnnie at her heels; the pony was quite used to making her own way without encouragement, but the boy enjoyed being out of the boat and stretching his legs. Haynes Lift Bridge loomed a short distance in front; Seph swung the stern of the boat in towards the towpath, and Jacob jumped across. He ruffled his younger brother's hair as he ran past him, dodged around the horse and on to the bridge; he crossed over it, and hauling on the chain dangling from the end of one balance beam he raised it to allow the passage of the entourage.

Glancing along the canal to where another lift-bridge crossed two hundred yards away, he saw that one swing up clear of the channel too; the slim blond-haired figure dangling from its chain waved a hand at him and he waved back: *Tha's 'Arold!* Moments later, he watched a mule appear along the far towpath, and then the shape of the deep-loaded *Dee* pass under the bridge; and then Johnnie and the pony passed him, the *Alice Rose* gliding under his own raised bridge seventy yards behind them.

Well clear of the bridge, Johnnie took Molly's bridle in hand and drew her to a halt; his father steered the boat out to the right-hand side of the channel, away from the towpath. As it drifted to a stop, the towline fell slack and dropped to the bottom of the canal in time for Libby the mule to squeeze past Molly while Johnnie held her tight against the hedge. The *Dee* floated through behind, over the sunken towrope, and then both mule and boat passed Jake in turn with an exchange of cheerful ''Ow d'yeh do's?' He stayed put, knowing that the *Avon* would not be far behind; looking around, he saw it just passing under the other bridge. Johnnie too stayed where he was, leaving the tow slack for the Kain's second boat to pass.

Along at Foxes Lift Bridge, Harold sat on the end of the balance beam, holding it open. He watched as first his father's boat and then his sisters' passed the *Alice Rose;* like Jake, he stayed there, holding the bridge open for the Camplings to pass. He heard Johnnie click his lips, starting Molly towards him again, and he saw the boat gradually pick up speed; then the pony was passing him, Johnnie grinning across the canal with a cheery ''Ow yeh doin' 'Arry?'

'H'okay, Johnnie – 'ow 'bout you?'

'Yeah, foine 'Arry! See yeh!'

The towline drew slowly by, and then the boat was approaching. He saw Seph at the tiller and his spirits sank; but then another head appeared over the cabin-top and looked around. A smile spread across Annie's face when she spotted him; she climbed out into the well beside her father and waved. Then the *Alice Rose* was gliding silently by; he waved and smiled back:

'Annie! 'Allo – 'ow are yeh?'

'Very well 'Arold – wha' 'bout you?'

'Oi'm foine, Annie. See yeh soon?'

'Oi 'ope so 'Arold!' Her smile and her reply put a tingle in his heart. His thoughts were interrupted by Seph Campling:

'You on yer usual, 'Arold?' He forced himself to focus:

'S'roight mister Camplin'. Ter Robinson's.'

'Moind 'ow yeh go, 'Arold.'

'Yeah – good luck mister Camplin'.' Seph turned away with a knowing smile; Harold let the bridge down onto its abutments again and hurried across to run after his boats. Halfway between the two bridges, he passed Jake coming in the opposite direction with a wave and a quick hello.

It was only half a mile to their destination; he slowed to a walk to follow the boats rather than run to get back aboard. He'd be there just as soon that way, and his thoughts were on Annie: *She really is quite pretty...* But then Seph's words struck him: *'Moind 'ow yeh go...'* Had that been meant as a quiet warning for him? It was something people said – but had Campling been warning him away from his daughter? Doubt assailed him; but he could do nothing about it either way. He'd have to be patient, wait and see what the future brought – but he knew that for the first time in his young life he felt drawn to a member of the opposite sex, even if he had little understanding of the ramifications of that attraction...

Then the two boats were tying up outside the tar works, and he was too busy to dwell on his feelings.

A week in, and as they had all supposed the war had brought no change to the round of their lives. Work on the canals went on the same as ever, even if the buzz of tension and excitement was evident all around them whenever they were in contact with people 'on the bank'. Men were talking about the war, about how long it would take to settle the various disputes, to bring the campaigns across Europe and the east to an end; young men were queueing up to join the armed forces, and Jake eyed them with envy. An expeditionary force from the British army had set sail for France, all bluster and bonhomie, expecting a swift victory and an equally swift return home; fighting in Belgium was intense as Germany tried to achieve a quick subjugation of France so that she could turn her attention to Russia; and the Royal Navy's Home Fleet was beginning to patrol from its base in Scapa Flow to try to prevent shipping destined for Germany from entering the Baltic Sea.

***

More weeks passed. Sunday the thirtieth of August saw the *Alice Rose* approaching Hawkesbury Junction where the Oxford and Coventry Canals meet, forever known to boaters as Sutton's Stop after a one-time local manager of the Oxford Company. A smile spread across Seph Campling's face as Molly drew the empty boat around the long turn on the approach to the stop-lock and the junction itself, just as the summer dusk was darkening into night; they were on their usual easy schedule to go a couple of miles towards Bedworth and Newdigate Colliery for the next load of coal at first light the next morning. Now a relaxed overnight stop and a beer in the Greyhound beckoned, which would be made even more pleasant since he'd spotted his brother's boat already tied against the bank near the shallow stop-lock.

'Lead on Annie! We'll tie agin the *Sarah.*' His daughter, leading the horse, looked around:

'Wha's that Pa?' She called back to him.

'Down by the lock! Tha's yer Uncle Siah's boat.'

'Oh roight! We'll breast oop on 'em, shall we?' He nodded vigorously:

'Tha's what Oi said!' She grinned over her shoulder, taking Molly's bridle to lead her past two other boats that stood between them and their intended mooring. Standing on the fore-deck, Jacob held the towline high to clear their chimneys, cans and masts; and then the *Alice Rose* bumped gently against the side of her sister-boat. He dropped the fore-end mooring line over the other boat's T-stud as his father did the same at the stern; they drew them tight and tied them off to secure them together. Annie unhitched the rope from Molly's harness; coiling it, she tossed it to her brother who laid it on the fore-deck, and then knowing what was required she led the pony away past the pub and so to the stables for the night.

The cabin doors of the *Sarah Ann* had swung open at the first contact between the boats. The slide hatch over them already stood open; the grizzled head of the older Campling brother appeared in the space, a grin spreading across his face. He didn't speak until Joseph had his boat secured, but then stepped up into the stern well behind his cabin and stuck his hand out:

'Seph – Oi thought as we'd mebbe see yeh ternoight.' Joseph took his hand and shook it enthusiastically:

'Yeah, good ter see yeh, Siah. You goin' ter load in the mornin'?'

'S'roight. You?'

'Yeah. Noodigate. You?'

'Pooley 'All, fer Banb'ry agen.'

'Ah. Goin' fer a beer?'

'Aye. Joannie's gettin' ready. You comin'?'

''Course! We'll get cleaned oop an' join yeh.'

Johnnie had stuck his head out of the cabin, but he was polite enough to wait while his father and uncle spoke; now he chipped in:

''Allo, Ooncle Siah!' Josiah gave the boy a grin:

''Allo there Johnnie! 'Ow are yeh, boy?'

'Oi'm foine, Ooncle Siah – 'ow are you, an' Auntie Joan?'

'We're all roight, Johnnie. Workin' 'ard, loike Oi 'ope you are too?' Johnnie glanced at his father:

'Yeah, Pa keeps oos at it! Don' get no rest, we don't.' Joseph aimed a playful swipe at the boy's head which Johnnie ducked, laughing:

'Can Oi come wi' yeh ter the pub ternoight, Pa? Oi don' see Ooncle Siah offen, do Oi?'

'We'll see Johnnie. Go get yerself clean an' toidy.'

'Yes, Pa!' The boy knew that that instruction heralded agreement to his request. He dived into the cabin for the handbowl to have a wash as his father told his uncle:

'We'll see yeh in there, Siah.'

'Roight.' Josiah nodded and ducked down into his own cabin again.

Chapter Five

Twenty minutes later Joseph led his wife and family into the small, cramped front bar room of the Greyhound. A number of other boaters were already gathered; Josiah beckoned them from beside the bar:

'What're yeh 'avin, Seph? Beth, Jake? Lemonade fer you two is it, Annie, Johnnie?' Eager nods from the youngest two heads accompanied Joseph's reply:

'Oi'll 'ave a pint o' mild, Siah. Stout fer Beth' She nodded her agreement 'An' a shandy fer Jacob?' Another nod:

'Yeah, thanks Ooncle Siah.'

As he turned to pay the landlord, Josiah waved a hand to the corner of the room:

'Joannie's got terday's paper, she'll read it out fer oos.'

'Yeah – 'urry oop an' get yer drinks, she's kep' oos waiting 'til yeh got 'ere!' The jocular request came from one of the other boaters, clutching his pint glass while he waited to hear the latest news. Joan held no illusion that it was her good looks or sparkling personality that made her a popular figure among the boating people, but her ability to read! Brought up in Banbury, the daughter of the local baker, Josiah Campling had wooed and then married her many years before, taking her away to become his wife and crew on the canal. Childless, nonetheless they enjoyed a happy and satisfying relationship, friends and companions as much as man and wife; anyone 'off the bank' was regarded with suspicion at first by the boaters, but she had soon settled to their way of life and become an accepted member of the boating community. That she was in fact popular among them, her reading notwithstanding, she would have pooh-poohed with a self-conscious smile.

She stood up to hug her nephews and niece, and kiss her sister- and brother-in-law as they gathered around the small table where she had spread out a copy of the Sunday Express. Resuming her seat, she looked around the throng of eager faces:

'D'you want to hear the news then?' A loud chorus of assent was over-ridden by her husband:

'Get on wi' it, woman!' She looked up at him, echoing the grin on his face, and then turned back to the newspaper.

'What d'you want first?' she asked without looking up.

'Tell oos 'bout the war Auntie Joan!' Jacob got his request in first, and no-one disagreed.

'All right! Well, there's been a big battle at sea...'

''Oo won?' Jacob wanted to know; she flapped a hand at him:

'If you'll be patient I'll tell you! Keep quiet and let me read it, Jake.' He subsided, chastened, as she quickly read the passage.

'The battle of Heligoland Bight...'

'Where the 'Ell's that?' Joseph asked. She flashed him an impatient look:

'You can keep quiet too, Joseph Campling! I'll tell you if you'll let me. It's up near Denmark, where the North Sea goes round into the Baltic – that's where the German ports are, you know? The Navy, our navy that is, sent some ships there to stop any freight getting through to Germany, and they attacked the German torpedo-boats and sunk a lot of them. But the Germans sent their bigger ships out and there was a bit of a fight, but we had reinforcements as well so they had to give up and run away. So it's one up to us!'

A round of applause greeted this news; Joan looked up with a grin before quickly reading another story:

'Things aren't so good in Belgium, though...'

'Wha's 'appened there?' She gave Jacob a withering look before going on:

'You know we sent our soldiers over to France to help stop the Germans attacking Belgium? Well, we didn't do so well. They've got us retreating – a strategic withdrawal, it says in the paper but it means we're having to back off however you read it! The French are having a good go at them, but they're getting the best of it at the moment. They're not far from Paris, and the French government have moved to Bordeaux out of the way.' She looked up again with a solemn expression: 'They aren't saying much, but it sounds like there've been an awful lot of casualties.'

'That's bad.' Josiah exchanged worried looks with those around him. Joan scanned on through the paper:

'And there's fighting going on in the east as well – the Russians are fighting the Germans in East Prussia as well as the Austrians in Galicia, and that's all a bit too-and-fro from what it says here.' She looked up again, concern clear on her face: 'I don't know about you all, but I don't like to think of all this fighting going on, men getting killed, for what? I suppose there were reasons, but it all seems kind of pointless to a simple soul like me!'

'It's got to be done, Auntie Joan!' Jacob seemed surprised at her reaction: 'An' any'ow, it'll all be over in no toime, that's what they said, ain't it?'

'Mebbe, Jake.' She didn't sound convinced.

'That it, Joannie?' her husband enquired; she nodded:

'All the important stuff anyway, Siah.' She leafed through the paper looking for other stories of interest to her audience as a buzz of conversation arose around her, everyone discussing the progress of the war.

Jacob drained his glass and dropped it on the bar. He knew his father wouldn't allow him a second shandy, and he didn't fancy being seen with a glass of lemonade in his hand; he strolled outside to where he'd previously spotted a few other teenagers off the boats leaning on the parapet of the curving bridge which spanned the turn where the two canals, the Oxford and the Coventry, met. Eddie Nolan waved to him from up there, and he walked around past the stables and up onto the arch to join them.

'Ello Jake! Yeh oop ter load termorrer?' Eddie enquired.

'Yeah, on ar usual run. You?' Nolans ran a pair of horse-boats for Harvey-Taylors of Aylesbury:

'Waitin' fer h'orders. We'll be oop ter Pooley or Bed'orth, then back ter h'Aylesb'ry basin Oi 'spect.'

'You 'eard 'bout ar Archie?' Jenny Grantham asked; Jacob shook his head:

'No - wha's 'e doon?'

''E's gorn an' joined the h'army!'

'Yeah? Lucky beggar!'

'Lot's o' boatees are joinin' oop' Eddie confirmed: 'Ar cousin Ken's gorn, an' Freddie Kendall.'

'Wish Oi could go wi' them.' Jacob sounded wistful.

'Me too' Eddie agreed: 'What a h'adventure, eh?' Jacob shrugged:

'Too ruddy young though, ain't we?'

'Yeah! Ken an' Archie an' them's all loike eighteen or older.'

'You can join oop when yeh're old enough.' Jenny consoled them, slipping an arm through Jacob's; he gave her a smile but shook his head again:

'All be long over an' done by that toime, won' it?'

Chapter Six

Their enthusiasm for the fight was far from unique in those early days of the war. Right across Europe and beyond, young men were queueing to take up arms in whatever patriotic cause they sought to join; there was even the feeling that Jacob had expressed, that if they didn't get there soon it would all be over. The concept of war that everyone held to was of battles joined, fought, won or lost and then broken off - that was how wars were conducted. Glorious conflict soon concluded, and to the victor the spoils. Even as the expected quick campaigns began to collapse into long-drawn-out back and forth struggles, the expectation of a rapid end to it all remained undiminished.

As the summer of 1914 descended into autumn and then slid slowly into winter, the fighting in France and Belgium went on. The German expectation of a quick victory which would leave their armies free to attack Russia had proved embarrassingly mistaken; they were fought to a halt along the River Marne, and then driven back by a fierce counter-attack mounted by the French and British armies. The western end of the extended front line wriggled its way gradually southwards even as it stalled in the east; the fall of Antwerp in October saw most of Belgium under German occupation, and then an offensive aimed at taking the Channel ports of Calais and Boulogne was again fought to a halt by mainly British forces around the town of Ypres. Snowfall in November saw the fighting cease, the opposing armies literally digging in for the winter - and so the first of what would become the infamous trenches appeared.

In eastern Europe too the fighting was intense between the Russian and Serbian armies and their German and Austro-Hungarian opponents, across the continent from Serbia to Poland. German strikes, successful in themselves, were frustrated by lack of supplies and reinforcements so that they were followed by withdrawal to a secure line; hampered as much by antiquated thinking as antiquated equipment, Austrian successes were few and far between. A stalemate ensued here too after a Russian attempt to invade Silesia, an important source of raw materials, was thwarted by the Germans under von Hindenburg. Similar back-and-forth struggles were going on around Turkey and Mesopotamia, with the British involved in the south.

But in the midst of all this world-wide conflict, life on Britain's canals continued as it had for generations. Many crews had lost older sons to the armed forces, but other than the grumbling about the harder work they left behind, their families carried on with their regular round, especially on the quieter waters of the Oxford road.

Early November, a bitter night with frost already riming the banks, and Harold Kain, as ever on lift-bridge duty, hauled on the chain of Belchers Bridge. A long straight stretch of water lay in front of them, returning empty again to Oxford; the only evidence of civilisation at this remote spot was the railway running alongside the canal. Libby the mule trudged past him, looking as disconsolate as he felt; the *Dee* followed moments later, accompanied by the rattling of a long train of covered goods wagons running behind him. He cupped his hands to call out over their noise to his father at the tiller:

'Pa!' Alfred looked around: 'We gonna stop soon?'

'Wha's oop boy, yeh 'ad enough?'

'Fer terday, aye! Oi'm froze!' Alf gestured ahead:

'Aynho Wharf do yeh?' Harold nodded eagerly:

'Roight-oh!'

He stayed in place, sitting on the bridge's balance beam, while his sister's boat also passed, and then let it drop back into place. Hurrying across to the towpath, he strode quickly along the half-mile to the village wharf, overtaking both boats before they could reach there. Taking Libby's bridle, he drew her to a halt where the *Dee* could slide in against the bank; his heart gave a little surge as he saw that the next boat, facing in the opposite direction, was the *Alice Rose*. Alf and Mary quickly had the boat secured to the bank; Janet let the *Avon* drift in alongside, and she and Vera dropped their lines across to tie the boats together.

The two youngest girls, huddled in their heaviest coats, led the mules across the road bridge to the stables behind the Great Western public house; Alf washed and changed into a clean shirt as Mary slipped into a blouse and long skirt. In the *Avon* Janet and Vera too quickly washed and changed, eager to meet friends in the bar and warm up in front of the pub's fire. As his parents stepped out onto the towpath, Harold slipped inside to wash and make himself tidy - he hadn't seen Annie around the boat and hoped she would be in the pub with her family. Established routine prevailed: Janet accompanied her parents and brother over to the Great Western while Vera stayed behind to see Susan and Emily settled into their beds. In the cold weather, she didn't have long to wait; unlike the summer, the cold dark evening held no fascination for the two girls and they were soon back, the mules settled for the night, fed and groomed:

'Coom on, you two! Inter bed, quick.' They needed little encouragement, soon down to their underclothes and wriggling together for warmth under their blanket on the side-bed.

In the cosy bar, a number of grimy railwaymen occupied one corner of the room, arguing noisily; from another, Joseph Campling saw the new arrivals and beckoned them over:

'Alf - Mary - 'ow are yeh? Jan - 'Arold - coom an' join oos.' Alf gestured to the bar and went to get his family a drink; Mary led the others across the room. Harold felt his heart sink - no Annie! He felt the urge to ask after her, but held his tongue, nervous of betraying his interest. The adults were exchanging the news of the canal, their recent trips and the price of fodder; then he heard Beth Campling mention a name he knew:

'Young Albert Nixon's gorn an' joined the Navy, did yeh know?'

'Oh aye? There's lots o' young'uns joined oop fer the war, aint't there' his father commented. Harold asked:

''Ow's it goin', anyone know?'

The railwaymen were drifting out, their after-shift drink done; one of them overheard and paused to reply:

'Yeh 'eard the latest? Bloody Germans 'ave shelled Whitby!' Everyone turned to stare at him:

'What?' Alf sounded scandalised.

'S'right! Two German ships fired at Whitby an' Hartlepool, yesterday. Layin' mines in the sea there an' all. Lots o' people hurt an' killed, there were.'

'The bloody nerve! Oi 'ope the Navy chased 'em off?'

'They'd run for it before they could get there' the man told them: 'but we'll get 'em back, you wait an' see!' He nodded to them and left to go home for his dinner. The boaters looked around at each other, appalled:

'Tha's awful!' Beth was shocked; Mary nodded her agreement:

'Shootin' at ordinary folks! Tha's not...' She was lost for words.

'Bloody barbarians!' Her husband wasn't; nor was Seph:

'Yeah - h'animals, tha's what they are!'

They settled to discussing the progress of the fighting in France, the landlord chipping in with news now that they were his only remaining customers. Harold sat, sipping at his glass of lemonade, feeling depressed - nothing seemed to be going right, and his barely-acknowledged hope of talking to Annie had been dashed...

A little later, as the families rose to return to their boats, he plucked up his courage:

'Mister Camplin' - 'ow's Annie, is she all roight?' Seph gave him a curious look, but he replied:

'She's foine, thanks 'Arold.'

'She's asleep in the boat, we 'ad a long 'ard day.' Beth sounded more sympathetic, almost amused at his question.

'Oh - roight.' He trudged along behind his parents as the made their way back over the bridge, his boots crunching on the frosted grass, hands in his pockets, his head down.

***

The following morning Harold was awake early, up, dressed for work and out of the cabin into the pre-dawn darkness while his mother brewed tea and sliced bread for their breakfast. The girls were all about as well, the little ones gone for the mules while the older ones also brewed up and got ready for the day's journey; today would see them to Oxford, through Isis Lock onto the river and to the gas works ready to load. He stood, his feet braced on the ragged edge of the towpath, his bottom against the side of the *Dee's* fore-end, his breath misting in the frosty air. He looked up at the sound of hooves, expecting to see his sisters; but a smile spread across his face:

''Allo Annie!' She smiled back at him, a little shyly:

''Allo 'Arold! You h'all roight?'

'Oi'm foine thanks - 'ow 'bout you?' She shrugged:

'H'okay. You ter h'Oxford agen?' He nodded:

'Yeah. Wha're you on?' She grinned:

'More beer fer Banb'ry! Then we're oop ter Wyken fer coal fer Hayfield wharf, fer a change.'

'Oh ah? That a reg'lar trip?'

'No - just 'elpin' out 'cause the brew'ry's got plenty fer now.'

'Oh, roight...' A shout from the stern of the *Alice Rose* interrupted them:

'Coom on Annie, le's be away!' She looked over her shoulder:

'Yes, Pa!' She turned back to Harold: 'Oi gotta go. See yeh soon, eh?'

'Yeah, Oi 'ope so!'

Her smile as she picked up the towline from her boat's fore-deck and hooked it onto the pony's harness made his heart give a quick flutter; he stepped up onto the flat deck of his own boats to lift her towrope clear as her father poled the *Alice Rose* out beyond the breasted Claytons. Molly leant into the tow, starting the loaded boat moving; as it picked up way, Harold used his own weight on the rope to keep it moving as it drifted past his boats, lifting the line over their masts and chimneys, finally releasing it as it cleared the sterns. Annie, walking behind the pony, looked back with a wave; he waved and smiled in reply.

'Yeh loike Annie, don' yeh?'   His mother remarked, standing the hatches. He shrugged:

'She's noice.' But he felt the flush rising to his cheeks, and heard his mother chuckle softly:

'Pretty girl, Annie Camplin'.'

'Mebbe.' He tried to sound non-committal, only to hear her chuckle again.

Chapter Seven

Night had fallen as the *Sarah Ann* ran south from Northbrook Lock. The stocky Dales Pony with his white feet trudged unconcernedly along the uneven towpath; a mile and a half to go, two bridges, past the old quarry, a long bend and they would tie for the evening's frivolity. Christmas Eve! Josiah Campling, leaning on his tiller, was looking forward to enjoying the warmth and companionship of the Three Pigeons, up the lane by Pigeon Lock; he'd swung an unusual trip to Juxon Street Wharf in Oxford by talking nicely to the traffic manager at Sutton's Stop. A couple of weeks before, his path had crossed with his brother's, and their shouted conversation had resulted in an intended rendezvous at the Pigeons to celebrate the holiday. Other boaters. they knew, would try to make the welcoming pub, and so a jovial evening was in prospect. They were later than he'd hoped, slowed by oncoming traffic heading for Banbury; but the delay only made the prospect of a roaring fire, a mug of beer and good company all the more attractive.

Half an hour later, they tied at the end of a line of boats on the towpath short of the lock. The *Alice Rose* was there before them, two boats along; between them lay a pair of Thomas Clayton's decked-over tanker boats, deep-loaded. The boat securely moored, he led Socks away to the pub's stables for the night, giving the pony a rather peremptory rub-down before leaving him; Joan tidied the cabin and changed into her floral dress for the evening, wrapping herself in her heavy serge coat for the short walk to the pub. Josiah slipped into his clean shirt and trousers; slipping an arm through his wife's they strode quickly off through the chill drizzle to the warmth of the bar-room.

There, they found Joseph and Beth with the children, Annie and Johnnie allowed along 'because it's Christmas!' The bar was full of boaters, and with his brother's family Josiah was pleased to see the Kains - friends from earlier years, their paths rarely crossed now since he had taken the Banbury run for Barlows two years before. The fun was already under way, the beer and stout flowing; someone was playing a melodion, and a part of the cramped floor space had been cleared for couples to engage in a little step-dancing. The children, Johnnie, Susan and Emily Kain, and a number from other boats, were in a group in one corner, chattering and playing together; Annie and Harold remained with their parents, but he noticed that they had contrived to sit side by side, squeezed into the bench that ran along one wall of the room, and were looking pleased with themselves. Until Alf intervened:

''Arold! Stan' oop an' let missus Camplin' sit down!' Harold glanced at his father, a crestfallen look on his face, but he did as he was told. Annie smiled up at him and hotched along a little to make room for Joan to slip into his place as Siah returned from the bar with a pint of mild and a glass of stout for his wife.

The talk revolved around families and festivities; no-one referred to the war going on across the seas in Europe and further afield, unless it was in mention of the absence of many of the younger men from boating families. At such comments Jacob, squeezed into a corner, a glass of shandy in hand, would flash an envious look at the speaker. Music, dancing, an occasional carol, and the evening slipped away. The younger children were packed away to bed; Vera dragged her little sisters off against their vociferous protests, and Annie got up to retrieve her younger brother:

'Come on Johnnie, toime fer bed!'

'Oh! Do Oi 'ave ter?'

'Yes yeh do! Go along boy.' Seph exerted his authority.

'Yes Pa. G'noight Pa, Mam; Uncle Siah, Auntie Joan.' Johnnie's shoulders were slumped in disappointment but he was as polite as ever. Annie took him by the hand:

'Come on - Oi'm goin' ter bed too.' She flashed a glance at Harold: 'G'noight, 'Arold, see yeh in the mornin'.'

'Er - yeah, see yeh Annie.'

'Soomthin' goin' on there, Beth?' Joseph had caught the undertones, and now he turned to his wife. She smiled, and he heard Mary Kain chuckle:

46

'Oi think ar 'Arold loikes yer daughter, Seph!   'E's been eyein' 'er fer a whoile.'

'What? She's only thirteen!'

'Fourteen now, Seph' his wife corrected him.

'Even so...' Mary laughed:

'Don' worry, Seph, there ain't nothin' to it! They're young.'

'Hnh! Mebbe so.'

The revelry went on into the small hours; in such a quiet rural spot the landlord paid little heed to the licensing laws at the best of times, and Christmas Eve had long been a night for the boaters to gather there. A lot of boating children had their sleep disturbed by the rocking of boats as their parents climbed unsteadily aboard, but soon settled again as quiet descended once more.

Christmas Day was the one day of the year when the boating community collectively took a day off. Whether this was in respect of the season or to allow hangovers to subside is, perhaps, questionable; either way, that Christmas Day, a Friday, saw the men and women of the boats tied by Pigeon Lock gradually emerge into the cold, clear daylight and gather over mugs of tea while they waited for the pub to open. Children played in the sunshine, chattering, laughing and comparing their gifts; grown-ups came together in groups to talk about life and work. The progress of the war crept in and took over their thoughts, and when the word went around that Joan Campling had a newspaper, people began to drift along the towpath to the *Sarah Ann.*

After a few false starts, when new arrivals kept asking her for the latest news, Joan sat tight for a while to allow all those who were interested to gather around; then she picked up the paper and read out the various articles about the fighting. The news was by then a couple of days old, but no-one really minded; and there was in fact very little fresh news anyway. Her listeners soon learnt that much of the fighting on the western front had subsided, the opposing forces entrenched where they had come to rest as the winter weather set in.

'Oi thought they said as it'd be done by Christmas?' Alfred Kain complained as she put the paper down. A mutter of assent ran through the crowd:

'S'roight - what went wrong?' Seph Campling wondered; theories were bandied about, but the discussion went nowhere in the absence of information. Siah summed it up:

'Well, they got it wrong, didn' they? Them as runs things. Oi wonder 'ow long it's gonna take?'

'They'll sort it out when the weather's better, Ooncle Siah!' Jacob, listening in, was still confident.

'Oi ain't so sure, boy. Should'a been over 'fore now.' Jacob grinned:

'Oi don' mind if it goes on a bit! Mebbe Oi'll get ter go an' join in if it goes on a while!'

'Not if Oi 'as anythin' ter do wi' it!' His father told him.

'Oh Pa! Everyone else's goin'!' Siah put a hand on his wife's arm:

'There was a bit 'bout 'ow many was gettin' killed, weren't there, love?' Joan nodded and leafed through the paper again:

'Yes - here it is. They've tried to add up the numbers - 'old on... They say as there's been tens of thousands killed, lots of French lads but plenty of ours too. And they reckon the Germans have lost even more than us...'

''Oo cares 'bout them? They shouldn'a started it!' Again a rumble of agreement went around.

'And the correspondent out there says it's been even worse out in the east, where the Russians are fighting the Germans and the Austrians' Joan went on.

'So 'oo's winnin'?' a voice from the back asked. Alf laughed:

'No-one, by the sound of it!'

'We're doin' all roight at sea - there was somethin' about a big battle a week or two ago.' Siah added.

'That's right' Joan confirmed: 'The battle of the Falkland Islands...'

'Where the 'Ell are they?' someone asked.

'In the South Atlantic - near South America. We sunk a whole German squadron of ships!' A cheer went up until she added: 'But they're saying here that it's a disgrace that their ships are still coming down and firing on towns on the east coast. If we can sink their ships out there, why can't we stop them nearer home, that's what they're asking.'

'Bloody roight too!' Alf grumbled.

'Well there ain't nothin' we can do 'bout it, is there?' Seph sounded a pragmatic note which was greeted with nods all round.

The conversation turned to speculation about the extra work for the boats which had begun to develop on some parts of the canal system as a result of the war, but everyone present was quite happy to be able to carry on with their regular contracts as they always had. Someone noticed the time; the men all strolled cheerfully away to enjoy a beer for Christmas lunch.

Alf looked around for his son, without success until Beth Campling told him to try the stables. There, he found Harold sitting on a hay-bale talking to Annie, who had volunteered to give both Molly and her uncle's pony a good grooming while they too had a day off:

'Yeh comin' ter the pub, 'Arold?'

'Oi dunno, Pa...'

''E'd rather stay an' talk ter Annie!' Emily called out, teasing her brother from the next stall where she and Susan were briskly brushing the coats of their mules.

'S'roight! 'E fancies 'er, Pa!' Susan joined in, and Harold rounded on them angrily:

'Ain't no such thing! We're friends, tha's all!' Annie looked at him, her eyebrows raised, an amused smile on her face:

'Oi'm about done 'ere, 'Arold' she told him: 'My mam will want me back fer lunch now.'

'Oh - h'okay. See yeh later, mebbe?'

'Mebbe!' Her smile expressed her hope; he smiled back...

'Come on boy! Oi'm gettin' thirsty.' Alf almost dragged him from the stable to the sound of Annie's amused chuckle.

Chapter Eight

In the hamlet of Thrupp, Frank Marston leant on the bar in the Boat Inn, surveying the deserted room in front of him. Six o'clock on a cold and wet February evening; the dull grey day had given way to a windy, drizzly darkness, and he had just unlocked the front door of the public bar, more in hope than expectation. A fire glowed softly in the grate, a pile of logs and the coal-bucket to hand for him to stoke it up as and when any customers appeared. Maybe one or two of the lengthsmen from the canal yard would drop in for a quick one before their dinners; local farm workers would be heading home to their own warm kitchens if they had any sense. No-one else was likely to show up until or unless any boats stopped over for the night there, and the boatmen wouldn't tie up until much later than this.

But as if to give the lie to his thoughts, the door suddenly banged open and Joseph Campling strode in.

'Hello, Seph! You're early - fed up with this miserable weather?' Campling shook his head:

'No, Frank; we'd keep goin' normally, yeh knows we needs ter get 'em ahead. It's ar Johnnie - 'e's poorly, an' Beth wondered if your missus would tek a look at 'im. She thinks it's just a bit of a cold, but - yeh knows 'ow the women are wi' their kids, she's worried in case it's the flu.' Frank's brow furrowed in sympathy:

''Course she will Seph, you know you only have to ask!' He turned away and called through into the back room: 'Edie! You got a minute? She'll be right through, Seph' he reassured the boatman: 'A pint while you're here?' Campling nodded:

'Aye. We'll stop 'ere now any'ow, t'ain't worth goin' on, 'specially wi' the weather loike this.' Frank took a glass and went to draw a pint of mild ale; he felt concerned for the family, knowing that Beth must be worried about the boy if they'd taken the step of stopping early to consult his wife. The boaters would usually work until late, travelling as far as possible in the day in order to reach their next destination and with it, their next pay-day.

Edie had trained as a nurse, and now she was only too happy to put her knowledge to use for the boaters with their occasional illnesses or injuries. She bustled in from the small room at the back of the bar, wiping her hands on a tea-towel:

'Sorry about that, I was just washing up. What's the trouble? Seph?'

'It's ar Johnnie, Edie, 'e's a bit poorly. Would yeh moind tekin' a look, just ter ease Beth's worries?'

'Of course not Seph, you don't have to ask! Where is he, in the boat?' She too knew that the boater wouldn't have stopped unless he was really worried about his son.

'Ah - in the cabin wi' Beth. Annie's teken Molly ter the stable an' Jake's toidyin' the boat, 'e'll be in fer a shandy any minute!' Frank grinned and turned for another glass; Edie nodded and ducked back into their private rooms for a coat. Returning, she gave the boatman a smile:

'I'll go and have a look at Johnnie. Back in a minute!' She hurried out. Frank put the empty glass ready on the bar and gave Joseph a reassuring smile:

'How are things otherwise, Seph? You're keeping busy?' Campling shrugged:

'So-so. Brew'ry's quiet, they ain't makin' so much beer at the moment. We're on coal fer 'Ayfield Wharf or Juxon Street 'alf the toime, an' that's gettin' less an' less too.'

'Mmm - I suppose you can understand it. With so many young fellows away to the war, there aren't so many to drink the beer!' His comment was facetious, but they both knew there was a level of truth to it as well.

'An' Barlows are sayin' as they're sendin' most o' the coal ter the fact'ries round Birnigum an' Coventry, there ain't so much ter spare fer people down this way.'

'But you're getting steady work?'

'Oh aye! Enough ter keep oos goin'.' He gave the landlord a perplexed look: 'Ar Jacob's still goin' on 'bout joinin' the h'army! Oi keep tellin' 'im 'e's too young...'

'He's what, fifteen?'

'Comin' on sixteen.'

51

'Well you're right, Seph.   They don't want boys til they're eighteen, not for the fighting anyway.'

'S'what Oi'm tellin' 'im!   But 'e says as 'ow some younger one's are joinin' oop an' gettin' away wi' it.   Jackie Barnet fer one - 'e's barely fifteen an' 'e got teken oop.   Jake reckons as 'e told 'em 'e were older, an' got away wi' it.'   Frank shrugged:

'They'll send him home when they find out, surely?'

'Oi s'pose so.   But it don' stop Jake goin' on about it.'   Seph gave him a slightly self-conscious look: 'Besoides - Oi don' wan' 'im ter go, Frank.   There's been talk of 'ow many of 'em's gettin killed an' h'injured - Oi don' wan' that fer my boy.'

'Of course you don't!   No father would, Seph.   With any luck it'll be over before he's old enough to go, you'll see.'

'Oi moight'a known you'd tek Pa's soide, mister Marston!' The teenager's jovial voice from the doorway had them looking around.

"Ow long you been listenin'?' his father sounded worried.

'Just walked in - whoy?'

'Don' matter.'   Seph turned back to his beer.   Marston poured lemonade into the spare glass, filled it up with beer from the barrel behind him:

'There you go, Jacob.'

'Thank yeh, mister Marston.'   He took a long draught: 'Oi was ready fer that!'

'Missus Marston's gorn ter 'ave a look at Johnnie' his father told him.

'Yeah, Oi saw 'er.   'E's been coughin' soomat awful, mister Marston. All day.'

'Don't worry Jake, Edie'll check him over.   Probably just a nasty cold.'

'Ah.   Wha's 'appenin' wi' the war mister Marston, d'yeh know?'   Marston smiled:

'I read the paper every day, Jake!   Not a lot, right now.   But the navy's stopped the Germans from shelling the east coast, had you heard that?'   Jacob shook his head, and the landlord went on: 'They sent a fleet from Scapa Flow to Rosyth, in Scotland, and when the German battlecruisers came over again Admiral

Beatty met them and gave them a good beating, sent them running for home!'

'That roight Frank? One to oos, eh?' Seph echoed his son's grin.

'Yes - a couple of weeks ago, Seph. But then the buggers torpedoed two ships, gave them no warning at all! A submarine, that was. Despicable, I call it. And two of their Zeppelins dropped bombs on East Anglia the other week.'

'That roight? Bloody uncivilised, ain't they?'

'What about in France, mister Marston? What's 'appenin' there?'

'Hardly anything, Jake. Our army's still stuck where they were before Christmas, the French and the Germans the same. The weather's been bad, so they've all just been waiting it out. They're living in trenches, dug in the ground, taking the occasional pot-shots at each other, getting nowhere.'

'People 'ave been sayin' 'bout fightin' all over the place Frank?'

'Yes, that's right Seph. In Poland and Galicia, the Germans and Austrians against the Russians and the Serbians. They're at a bit of a stand-off too at the moment; there's been reports of them using poison gas even! And then in the Middle East, we're up against the Turks - they tried to take the Suez Canal but we stopped them.'

'*Suez* Canal? Never 'eard of it!' Frank laughed:

'It's a big canal, for ships! Between the Red Sea and the Med, let's them get from places like India and the East, bringing our supplies through. If we lose it they'd have to go all the way around Africa, that would take weeks longer.'

'Oh - roight.' Joseph still sounded confused.

''Ow much longer d'yeh reckon it'll go on, mister Marston?' Jacob asked.

'Who knows, Jake! Wasn't over by Christmas, was it? Once the weather gets better and they can get to it again hopefully we'll see it resolved before too long.'

'Oh - yeah.' Jake sounded disappointed, and Marston laughed:

'You really want to go and find yourself stuck in a muddy trench getting shot at?' Jacob shrugged:

'Oi just wants ter do me bit.'

The door opened and the landlord's wife came in, closing it hurriedly behind her. Joseph looked around:

"Ow is 'e, Edie?'

'Poor little fellow! He's got a nasty cough right enough, but I think it's only a bad cold. He's always had a bit of a weak chest, hasn't he?'

'Mebbe so.' Joseph was reluctant to admit to weakness in his offspring and she smiled at him:

'It's one of those things, Seph. He'll be all right, I'm sure! I've told Beth to keep him in the warm for a few days, let him get over it away from the cold and the damp. And I've got half a bottle of cough-mixture somewhere you can have for him.'

'Thank yeh, Edie, it's roight koind o' yeh.'

'Not at all, Seph, I'm happy to help.'

'We're on ar way ter Banb'ry now, then ter the coaleries. Oi'll drop yeh off a coupl'a buckets o' coal when we coom by next.'

**

The next week he was as good as his word. The *Alice Rose* paused outside the pub and Joseph took the old beer barrel that Marston stored the coal for his fires in and shovelled it full to the brim. Rolling it on its edge across to the back yard, he was met by Edie Marston:

'Oh, Seph! You didn't need to do that!'

'Oi don' break moy promises, Edie.'

'I know Seph - thank you. How's Johnnie now?' Joseph gave her a grin:

'Mooch better, thank yeh! 'E's still coughin' a bit, but not 'alf as mooch as 'e was.' He hesitated: 'Reckon as yeh was roight - 'e's got a bit of a chest, ain't 'e? Poor little beggar.'

'He'll be just fine, Seph! He's a lovely boy, you just need to look after him as he's growing up. Lots of kids have the same thing, and they usually grow out of it in time.' Joseph grinned again:

'As if 'is mam would let me do anythin' else! We'll tek care of 'im, never fear.' Edie smiled:

'You won't get into trouble, losing some of your load?' He chuckled:

'It's been rainin'! Got it wet, so they won' notice the diff'rence. It's fer Juxon Street any'ow, they ain't so fussy there.'

Chapter Nine

A pleasant Friday night in May. Joseph Campling was looking forward, as ever, to a pint of beer and a chat with friends as they tied the *Alice Rose* against the towpath opposite Enslow Wharf. Their cargo was for Oxford as usual, but their regular schedule had long gone by the board with the changing traffic patterns - less and less coal was destined for domestic use,which represented the majority of the loads on the southern Oxford Canal, although by combining that with the supply for Morrell's Brewery he had maintained a steady workload. They wouldn't make Hayfield Wharf until mid-morning the following day, and he knew they would be lucky if the boat was unloaded before nightfall - which would mean a delayed departure, until Monday.

Annie led the pony away, over the bridge to the pub stables; Johnnie, full of beans again after a prolonged illness - his bad chest had lasted some weeks - ran alongside her, chattering gaily. Seph and his wife secured the boat and then retired to the cabin for a wash and brush-up. Fifteen minutes later, they strolled across the road bridge with Jacob, and into the bar of the Rock of Gibraltar.

As he closed the door, Joseph looked around; a strange atmosphere had greeted them, a feeling of restrained anger hanging in the air:

''Allo folks - wha's oop?' Jim Nixon picked up a newpaper from the bar and brandished it - he might not be able to read it, but he knew now what news it held:

''Aven't yeh 'eard?'

''Eard? 'Eard what?' Nixon held the paper up, displaying the photograph on the front page - a huge ocean liner with four funnels:

'They sunk it!'

'What? That ship there?' Heads nodded around him; the barman took up the story:

'Torpedoed it. No warning, they just sunk it, like that. Near Ireland.' Joseph stared around at the angry faces:

'What ship is it?'

'The *Lusitania*. Cunard liner - she were coomin' back from 'Merica, with lots o' people on board. 'Undreds of 'em are dead, drownded.' Nixon sounded scandalised.

'Just - ord'nary folks? Not soldiers or nothin'?'

'H'ord'nary folks, Seph. Not just men neither - there was women an' kiddies on 'er too.'

'Oh, Seph!' Beth almost sobbed the words into the silence. Joseph led her over to the bar, pushing through the crowd:

'Gi's a pint, mate? An' a stout fer the missus, an' a shandy fer Jacob, eh?' A mutter of conversation rose around them as the barman poured their drinks; Seph took a long drag at his mild before turning around:

'Wha's the Navy doin' about it?'

'They say they're out searchin' fer the boat what did it. But they reckon as it were one o' them U-boats.'

'U-boats?'

'It's what the Jerries called their submarines.   Short for 'submarine' in German.' the landlord told him.

The silence that fell was brittle with anger.   Jacob took a swig from his glass:

'Goes ter show - we ought ter get stoock in an' stop 'em 'fore they does any more.' His father turned a frown on him:

'You on about goin' an' joinin' oop agen?'

'Pa! Oi'm nearly sixteen! Ev'ryone as can ought ter go an' fight 'em, don' yeh think?' He looked around for support; a few nodded, but others gave him an uncertain glance and looked away. It was Jim Nixon who spoke up again:

'Fifteen are yeh Jake?'

'Not fer mooch longer, mister Nixon!'

'Ah. Yeh 'eard about Jackie Barnet?'

'Yeah! 'E went an' joined oop, didn' 'e?'

'Aye. Kidded 'em 'e were seventeen, an' they never checked oop. Did 'is trainin' then they give 'im a rifle an' sent 'im ter France, las' month.'

'Lucky beggar!' Nixon eyed him for a moment:

'That ain't all. 'Is mam got the telegram two days ago.'

'Telegram?' Jacob sounded suddenly wary; his mother caught her breath and put her arm around Seph.

'Aye. Jackie got killed, at a place called Wipers. Never saw 'is sixteenth birthday.' Jake stared at him, his eyes wide, lost for any reply. Beth gave a sob and turned her face into her husband's jacket; Seph looked at his son as the boy slowly turned to him:

'Oh, Pa...'

'Oi don't wan' that fer you, son.' Jake shook his head, tears rising to his eyes; they all knew the Barnet family, a regular Barlows crew, had worked with them, drunk and laughed with them. Jake had played with Jackie as young boys; the image of his laughing face rose to wipe away his enthusiasm for the war:

'Pa...' He threw his arms around his father's neck, the tears now running down his cheeks; Seph put his spare arm round his waist:

'This foightin's fer proper soldiers, men as know what they're doin'. Not part-toime h'amateurs loike oos or young Jackie, eh?'

'Mebbe yeh're roight, Pa.' Jake spoke into his father's coat, his voice muffled; he lifted his head: 'Mebbe we ought ter see if we can foind work that'd help the war? Look fer loads that'll do soom good, not just coal fer folks' foires?'

'Ah, mebbe we could at that, boy. Let's think about it, eh? Fer now we got a job ter do, roight?' Jake nodded:

'Yes, Pa.'

As they embraced, Annie had come into the pub with her younger brother:

'Wha's oop Pa? Mam?' Jacob let go of his father and walked over to them; he took one in each arm:

'It's Jackie, Jackie Barnet. Yeh remember 'im? 'E's been killed, in France.'

'Oh Jake! Tha's awful!' Annie reached up to put her arms around his neck, remembering that the two boys had been friends; Johnnie just looked up at his brother, sadness in his eyes. For that moment, the personal tragedy of the boating community overrode the greater tragedy at sea for those in the hushed bar.

For all of the gathered crowd, the loss of one of their own served to add poignancy to their fury at the sinking of the great liner, a symbol of British pride. The huge loss of life had stirred them, but those losses were impersonal. While the Campling family huddled in a corner of the bar, trying to soften Jacob's shock and pain, everyone else fell to discussing the farther-flung progress of the war as it was related to them by the landlord.

May 1915: Of most interest to the boaters, as to the British people generally, was the Western Front, the fighting in France and Belgium; here, hostilities had begun again as the spring approached in north-eastern France and around Ypres. The German use of gas also aroused anger among his listeners, their mood not improved by the lack of any real progress from Allied counter-offensives. News from the Middle East was no better - the landings at Gallipoli intended to secure passage for allied shipping to and from the Black Sea had stalled. And in the east the German forces were pushing the Russians back; there seemed to be little to celebrate, and the mood in the bar that night was sombre altogether.

Chapter Ten

The evening sun struck low across the river channel and sparkled orange on the rippling water of the basin as it tumbled from the paddles of Isis Lock. On the bank below, Vera Kain hung onto the back-end line, holding the *Avon* against the side while Buddy stood patiently waiting to haul the boat into the lock; her two younger sisters stood ready to swing the gates back as soon as the weight of the water came off of them. Janet and Harold stood by the top paddles, windlasses in hand; their parents with the *Dee* had just disappeared around the turn into the canal channel, Libby leaning into her harness to get the heavy-loaded boat moving.

Late July - their trips went on as ever, although since the spring they had found themselves often kept waiting to load at Oxford's gas works. Two trips a week had declined to three in the fortnight, and threatened to get even less as production at the works was cut back further. Alf was concerned, his income down in proportion, but he kept his worries to himself although he could see the same thoughts behind his wife's eyes; his son's dark mood had quite another basis. They'd not seen the Campling family for some time - usually their paths would cross quite regularly so that he would get to exchange a greeting with Annie as their boats passed even if they had no opportunity for a proper conversation, and he found himself missing the sight of her pretty, smiling face.

Suey had taken up the habit of teasing him about Annie, accusing him of fancying her, knowing that he would rise to the bait every time, angrily denying any such interest in her: 'We're joost friends, tha's all!' But recently she had given it up, realising that he really was upset about not seeing her and secretly smiling at the accuracy of her guess.

Buddy stomped slowly past him as the *Avon* swam into the shallow lock; he whipped up his paddle, raised a hand to his eldest sister and turned to run off up the towpath after the *Dee*. If he caught up with them he could ride for a while - the first of the close succession of lift-bridges didn't start until Frenchay

Bridge, almost a mile away, and the first lock would be Wolvercote, more than two miles off. It was getting late anyway, and he was hoping that his father would stop soon, maybe at the Plough on Wolvercote Green.

Alf caught sight of his son from the corner of his eye and swung the stern of the boat in close to the towpath. Harold jumped the gap, landing easily on all fours on the planked deck of the boat in front of the cabin; he stepped up onto the cabin-top and walked across it, jumping down into the well beside his father and sitting on the gunwale at the side:

''Ow far we goin', Pa?'

'Not far, 'Arold. Wolvercote mebbe, ain't no need ter 'urry these days.' That was as close as Alf had come to admitting his thoughts about their declining trade and Harold nodded, sensing his father's concern. He sat in silence, enjoying the peace of the summer evening as they passed the wharf at Juxon Street, strangely quiet with the loss of much of the domestic coal traffic to Oxford. The tall buildings of Lucy's Iron Foundry began to loom over them on the right, the open land on their left the beginnings of what would become Port Meadow as they travelled on, only the railway intruding on its expanse. A boat was unloading coal into the works, at an open dock let into the side of the building; he peered at it, idly curious to see who it might be.

Alf looked around as his son got to his feet, a smile beginning to spread across his face:

'Look Pa! It's Camplin's!' Alf followed his son's gaze and chuckled:

'So 'tis boy! Ain't seen them fer a whoile, 'ave we?'

'S'roight Pa. Shall oos stop an' see 'em?' Alf looked at the boy:

'Dunno.' He saw Harold's face fall, and laughed: 'Dolly's 'Ut do yeh? Mebbe they'll meet oos there eh?'

They were drawing close now, and could see Joseph and his eldest son shovelling the coal into barrows inside the boat. Beth wheeled one up onto the dockside and turned to take it inside the factory; moments later, Annie followed with a second. Spotting the mule on the towpath, she looked around and saw the approaching boat; dropping the handles of the barrow she waved to them before taking it up again and disappearing within the building.

Joseph rested his shovel and wiped his brow on his sleeve as the *Dee* rode past:

'Alf! Good ter see yeh mate! An' you 'Arold - you h'okay?'

'We're foine Seph - you be done ternoight?'

'Nah - barely 'alf empt yet, we'll be 'ere overnoight. Where yeh stoppin'?'

"Ow bout we see yeh in Dolly's 'Ut in a whoile?'

'Yeah, that'd be good! Oi've 'ad enough o' this fer ternoight - 'alf an hour?'

'See yeh there!'

Beth had emerged again and overheard the conversation; she raised a weary hand to them in greeting. Annie appeared behind her and waved both hands eagerly:

''Allo 'Arold! You h'okay?' He waved back, grinning widely:

'Yeah, you?' She nodded and he added: 'See yeh oop Dolly's 'Ut!' Her nod and smile grew even more eager as the boat drew on past.

Five minutes later Harold stepped off the *Dee* with the back-end line as his father steered into the towpath opposite Hayfield Wharf. His sisters brought the *Avon* to a halt behind them, the channel there too narrow to allow them to breast the boats together; Susan and Emily collected the mules and led them across Aristotle Bridge to the wharf and the stables for the night while their parents and older siblings secured and tidied the boats before quickly washing and changing into their stepping-out clothes. Harold got an indulgent smile from his mother and a quiet chuckle from his father as he took great pains over brushing his thick blond hair, and then they were setting off together to cross the bridge.

The Anchor public house on Hayfield Road had been known to the boaters as Dolly's Hut since time immemorial, and served as their meeting place in that part of Oxford. Night had fallen as Alf walked with his wife and son and eldest daughter up Aristotle Lane, across the road and into the busy, smoky room. Boating acquaintances greeted them from all around as they made their way to the bar; Alf was digging into his pocket to pay for their drinks as the door opened again and Seph Campling and his family walked in.

'Seph! Over 'ere mate - what're yeh 'avin'?' They made their way across to join him:

'We ain't stoppin' long Alf - gotta be oop ter finish unloadin' in the mornin'.' Alf grinned:

'Yeh can get oos one back another day, mate! It's good ter see yeh.'

'H'okay! Thanks Alf. Usual.'

Drinks in hand, the two families congregated in a corner of the room, Beth and Mary squeezed into a small bench, the others standing on the sawdust-strewn floor.

'Yeh walked 'ere?' Alf enquired.

'Yeah - t'ain't far, oop Southmoor Road an' Kingston Road. We'd'a mebbe gorn ter the Gardener's if yeh 'adn't coom along; Victoria's too 'oity-toity, they don' want boatees in there! Fella in there 'ad a go at ar Jake las' toime, said as 'e ortta be orf foightin'.'

'Yeh put 'im roight?'

'Oh ah!' Seph laughed: 'Tol' 'im we was keepin' the fact'ries goin'. But Jake didn' loike it.'

''E still goin' on about joinin' oop?' Seph shook his head:

'Nah, not so mooch. Still thinks as 'e ortta be doin' more ter 'elp, but when young Jackie got killed it took the wind out of 'is sails a bit. 'Im an' Jackie was good mates.'

'Jackie Barnet? Yeah, we 'eard about it. Bloody shame, 'e were a noice kid.' A brief silence commemorated the boy they'd all known.

'They're askin' fer more men ter join oop, 'ad yeh 'eard?' Seph asked.

'Yeah - there's fellas goin' orf the boats, the young'uns, as we know. Yeh keepin' busy?' He changed the subject:

'Yeah - we ain't this way mooch though. Mostly been on coal ter the fact'ries in Coventry lately. They're all on war work, an' they needs it more'n folks at 'ome. We've been 'ere ter Lucy's a coupl'a toimes.' Alf nodded:

'Wi' the coal the fact'ries need the gas works ain't doin' so mooch, means we ain't gettin' the loads neither.'

They fell to discussing the trade and conditions on the canal. Sitting in the corner, their wives were talking families as mothers will the world over:

'Johnnie asleep in the boat?' Mary asked, and was surprised when Beth shook her head:

'We left 'im wi' 'is grandma in h'Oxford fer a whoile. 'E 'ad a real nasty cough fer ages in the winter, an' it keeps coomin' back. Oi'm 'opin' it'll get better properly if 'e 'as some toime on the bank. An' grannie Camplin's goin ter send 'im ter school whoile 'e's there! We'll 'ave a scholard in the fam'ly wi' a bit o' luck!'

'Tha's got ter be good, Beth - be better fer 'im later, eh?'

'We 'opes so, Mary. 'E's a broight kid, won' do 'im no 'arm any'ow. Seph ain't convinced, moind, but 'e's h'okay wi' leavin' 'im there fer a whoile so's 'e can get better.'

The teenagers were in their own little gaggle; Harold found himself squeezed against Annie, and caught between feelings of joy and embarrassment. Annie seemed to be far more relaxed about it, smiling cheerfully at everyone as she joined in the conversation about the progress of the war; Jake had been explaining his change of heart:

'Jackie an' me was real good pals, yeh know? It kind o' makes yeh think agen when someone as yeh knows gets killed, just loike that. Oi mean - Oi still wants ter do me bit ter 'elp, but what's the use in gettin' killed? 'Alf of me wants ter go an' foight still, but...'

'We are doin' ar bit, Jake' his sister told him: 'Loike Pa says, we're keepin' the fact'ries goin' so's they can make the guns an' bullets an' stuff. An' without ar Johnnie there's only you an' me an' Mam an' Pa - if you went orf it'd be 'ard work fer oos.'

'Yeah Oi know! Yeh'd manage without me - but since Pa got oos on the fact'ry trips Oi feel as we are 'elpin' things along.'

'Tha's roight' Harold agreed: 'Wha' d'you think Jan?' He asked his eldest sister, standing with them but keeping her thoughts to herself:

'They needs men ter go an' foight, Oi s'pose - but not at your age, Jake. Nor you, 'Arold! An' Oi 'ope as it'll all be over before either of you are old enough ter go.'

'You sixteen now, Jake?' Vera had joined them after seeing the girls to bed.

'Yeah, s'roight.'

'An' 'Arold's only just fifteen, too young ter join the h'army...' She paused: 'Too young ter get killed, loike poor Jackie, roight? Can yeh h'imagine 'ow 'is folks feel?' They too held a silence for a moment.

'They're usin' h'aeroplanes now! Did yeh know?' Harold let his amazement show in his voice.

'Yeah, so someone tol' oos' Jake confirmed.

'What use are they?' Annie asked.

'They use 'em over the foightin', ter tell 'em where ter h'aim the guns' Jake told her.

'An they send 'em oop ter stop the Zeppelins an' all!' Harold added.

'That'd be a way o' joinin' in without gettin' killed, wouldn' it?' Jake said thoughtfully; they all looked at him:

'Yeah, mebbe...'

'One o' the men at the gas was sayin' as 'ow a lot o' women are complainin' that they can' do more towards the war' Janet said thoughtfully: ''E said as they 'ad a big march in Lunnon about it th'other day.'

'Oh? You gonna join the h'army then Jan?' Jake asked her with a laugh; she shook her head, grinning:

'Nah! They don' want ter foight, yeh silly beggar! But they could work in the fact'ries mebbe, or things like that. Do 'em good, a lot o' them, Oi reckon - we 'as ter work, don' we Vera?'

'Yeah! Get 'em out o' their fancy 'ouses doin' somethin' useful, eh?' But the thoughtful look was still on Janet's face.

Chapter Eleven

Henry Scott looked at the message he'd just been given and read it through with a growing sense of loss. It was intended for Alfred Kain, a man he had always got along well with, and its import was clear to him even if it was not actually stated.

Henry was a foreman at Robinson Brothers Ltd, the Banbury company who received the gloop created in the production of town gas from coal and distilled it, the various fractions thus separated being then turned into useful by-products like oils and soaps. He'd been taken on in 1912, when the works opened, and all that time the boats delivering their raw material from the Oxford gas works had included Alfred's pair; the two men had quickly come to respect each other even if to call them friends would be overstating the case a little. But now the message he had to deliver meant, he knew, that another boatman would be taking over that trip, and he would miss the easy-going relationship he'd enjoyed with Alf.

It was a bitter December morning, a mist hovering over the canal outside as he walked out onto the wharf, even a thin skim of patchy ice covering the water. He looked towards Oxford, but saw no sign yet of the boats approaching - their departure had been delayed yet again, waiting for a decent load. Gas production, and hence the volume of residues for them, had been declining slowly for some time, largely due to the number of homes and businesses switching over to what Henry still thought of as 'that new-fangled 'lectric light'. But since the war started, it had been going down at a greater pace than ever as coal supplies were appropriated for the manufacturing industries. They had been receiving some extra supplies from elsewhere, an occasional load from Leamington Spa, but even so their own production had been quite badly hit.

***

A mile to the south, out of sight from Robinson's wharf, Harold Kain sat on the end of the balance beam of Haynes

66

Bridge. Ice tinkled under the fore-end of the *Dee* as it floated past him, Libby pacing easily along seventy yards in front; he was panting after the run along the towpath from Foxes Bridge, having sat there while both boats passed him and then had to hurry to get to this one in time to raise it before his father got there. Alf gave his son a grin from the tiller; a minute later Buddy tramped by, her towline stretching back to the mast of the *Avon;* once his sisters' boat was past he dropped the bridge onto its abutment, ran across and set out to walk the half-mile to Robinson's factory, not worrying about reboarding the boat for such a short distance.

He arrived in time to help tie the two boats side-by-side on the wharf; then the wharf hands helped as he and his father opened the hatches in the decks to allow access to the oily cargo within. The suction hoses were run out and fed into the holds with the hissing steam hoses needed to liquify the tarry residues, the pumps started, and then Henry took advantage of the time to talk to Alf, after the usual exchange of pleasantries:

'I've got a message here for you, Alf, from the office at Brentford.'

'Oh ah?'

'Yeah - they want you to go to Leamington Spa gas works and load there, and then go to Oldbury. Unload at Springfield Works, then go to the yard.'

'What about ar trip 'ere?'

'It says they're sending a guy called George Bellingham to do that.'

'Oh...' Alf was clearly unhappy: 'Whoy is it, do they say?'

'They want to dock your boat, it says.'

'Hnh - well Oi s'pose it's 'bout toime, we've 'ad it fer nigh on foive year now. They got another one fer oos?'

'Doesn't say, Alf. But they will, surely?'

'Oh yeah, bound to. Be noice ter know what boat though.' He shrugged: 'Oi guess we'll see when we gets there.'

'Does this mean we're losing you, Alf?' The boatman drew a breath through his teeth:

'Probably, 'Enry. Wi' the loads gettin' less an' less, mebbe they're goin' ter run a single boat on this trip. Ar two'll be sent somewhere else, Oi 'spect.'

'I'll be sorry to lose you, Alf. Do you know this Bellingham guy?' Alf laughed:

'Oi should! 'E's Mary's ooncle - she were a Bellin'ham 'fore Oi married 'er, 'er Pa was George's brother. 'E passed away a coupl'a years ago. Yeh'll get on foine wi' George, 'e's' a decen' fella.'

'That's good to know, Alf. You'll keep in touch?' Alf smiled:

'Oi'll do me best, 'Enry. Mebbe we'll get another trip down this way, eh?'

The two shook hands, and Henry walked away to supervise the unloading; Alfred called his family together:

'We're goin' ter h'Ol'bry. Loadin' at Leamin'ton Gas on the way, then ar boat's goin' on the dock; Oi don' know yet what we'll be on after that.' Mary and his children took this in in silence, exchanging glances that ranged from the sad (Mary) to the excited (Emily) and everything in between. As they all separated again to watch the conclusion of the unloading, the two youngest girls rushing off to play together, Janet and Vera walked with their father:

'Pa?' Janet spoke tentatively; he turned to her:

'Yes Jan?'

'We've been wonderin', Vera an' me, if mebbe we ortta foind oos jobs in one o' the gun fact'ries or soomat. Go an' do soomat fer the war, yeh see?' She raised her hands to hold off his protests: 'You an' Mam could manage the boats, wi' 'Arold and Suey an' Emmie, now they're gettin' older, yeh don' really need oos any more. An' we think as we ortta be doin' soomat - we can' go an' foight, not as we'd want ter! 'Arold's too young ter go, an' we wouldn' want 'im ter any'ow. This way we could be doin' soomat - as a fam'ly, loike?'

Her speech had taken the wind out of his sails; he regarded her with a slightly annoyed expression:

'Yeh've got this all thought out, ain't yeh?' She chuckled:

'Yes, Pa!' He stood in thought:

'Let's talk 'bout it when we gets ter h'Ol'bry. Gi' me a chance ter think 'bout it, h'okay?'

'H'okay Pa!' He turned way with a grunt, but she caught the smile on his face as well.

***

That Friday saw the two empty boats up onto the summit of the Oxford Canal; delayed by ice building up behind lock gates for much of the day, they tied near Fenny Compton wharf for the night, taking advantage of the welcoming coal fire of the George & Dragon Inn and its well-kept ales. Saturday - milder weather, and down the nine locks to Napton village, and then a left-hand turn onto the Warwick and Napton canal and a continuing descent, every lock worked twice to pass each boat in turn. Thus into the Avon Valley, taking it easily as the works would not load them on the Sunday, to a tie close by Royal Leamington Spa Gas Works in the early evening. With no work on Sunday, Alf had them all hard at it getting both boats into spectacularly pristine condition, eager to make the best possible showing when they returned to the company's main base in Oldbury a few days later. In the afternoon the whole family sought out the town's public baths and enjoyed a thorough scrubbing themselves.

They were loaded early on the Monday, away in mid-morning for the trip into Birmingham: Through Warwick and up Cape Two and the twenty-one locks of Hatton flight;   a few miles on the level before the left-and-right junction onto the northern Stratford-on-Avon Canal straight into another nineteen locks of Lapworth. At last able to relax, they tied that night below the Bluebell Inn at Warings Green; the following day saw them at the Springfield Tar Works beside the Old Main Line of the Birmingham canals, joining a queue of other Clayton boats waiting to unload.

Before midday on Wednesday, empty once again, they tied the boats on the Oldbury yard which was Thomas Clayton Ltd's

Birmingham base and the centre of its Midland operations. Alf set out to find out where the company wanted his boat, and what their change boat was to be; half an hour later he was back, strolling across the yard in company with another Clayton boatman to inform his wife:

'We gotta take ar boat ter Fellers's dock at Saltley, roight away. They got a new'un there fer oos, the *Tiber*, ready ter go.'

'Well, t'ain't new' his companion put in: 'Joost off'n the dock though. Oi 'ad it before - it's a good'un, yeh'll loike it. Oi've got the *Kennet* now.'

'Yeh knows Jim Tolley?' Alf asked his wife; Mary laughed:

'O' course! 'Ow are yeh Jim? 'Ow's Liz, an' the kiddies?' The man chuckled:

'We're all foine Mary, thanks! They're all off ter the baths whoile I'm waitin' on a new 'orse - ar old'un got taken lame yestiday. Good 'orses are gettin' ard ter coom by, they keeps takin' 'em fer the h'army.'

'S'roight - Oi'm glad we got ar two ol' mules, they'll keep oos goin' fer years yet' Alf commiserated: 'What're yeh on, Jim?'

But before the boatman could reply, a smartly-dressed man in his late fifties approached them, his heavy coat drawn about his shoulders, a homburg hat pulled down over his greying hair, and they turned to greet him deferentially:

'Good mornin' mister Thomas.' Alf tipped his own hat to the man; Tolley followed suit as Thomas Clayton himself held out his hand:

'Mister Kain - we haven't seen you here for a while! Mary - Mister Tolley - everything all right with you?' They shook hands with the company managing director in turn:

'We're all foine thank yeh mister Thomas, joost waitin' on a new 'orse' Tolley repeated.

'How about you, mister Kain? Any problems?'

'No sir - Oi'm takin' the *Dee* ter Saltley fer dockin', pickin' oop a change boat there.'

'You've been paid for the trip from Leamington?'

'Oh yes!' Alf pulled a small brown envelope from his jacket pocket, and Clayton laughed:

70

'Not opened yet? You're very trusting, Alfred! You'll find that we've paid you a day's laying money for today, while you change your boat, and three days empty running to get you to Northampton.'

'Thank yeh! That's very koind o' yeh, mister Thomas.'

'It's not your fault we've called you up here, Alf, and your family have to live! You'll be off to Saltley shortly?'

'Any toime, sir, joost waitin' fer the girls ter get back from the shops.'

'Right - you have your orders after that?'

'Yes sir - we're goin' ter Northampton, ter do the run from there ter 'ere.' Clayton nodded:

'That's good. I'm glad I caught you, Alfred - we're sorry to take you off of the Oxford traffic, but as you'll have realised there isn't the trade there now for two boats. The Northampton trip takes much longer, so it makes more sense to have you on that run - they'll have enough tar to load a pair of boats on each trip, better for you and for the company!' Alf nodded:

'Yes, Oi can see that sir.' He hesitated: 'Mister Thomas - could yeh 'elp me out. Mebbe?'

'If I can, Alfred - what is it?'

'Well sir - moy two girls, Janet an' Vera, they wants ter foind work on the bank, ter do soomat fer the war yeh see. Oi've still got the missus, young 'Arold an' the two young'uns ter work the boats, an' - well they're real keen ter do it...' Clayton nodded:

'I see Alfred - I'll see what I can do. I know they're crying out for people in some of the factories, I'm sure we can find a job for them! We're pretty desperate for boatmen ourselves, so many have left to join the army or the navy since this all started - I'm increasing the rates we pay for you all to try and attract new crews. Maybe I could talk them into taking on another boat? Under your captaincy of course?'

'That's koind o' yeh, mister Thomas - but they're dead set on doin' this war work. Mebbe once it's all over they'll coom back on the boats - that's what Oi'm 'opin' fer any'ow.'

'All right Alfred - Let me see what I can do. You'll be at Saltley later today?'

'Yes sir.'

'Right - I'll try to get a message to you there if I can.' He smiled and held out his hand again: 'All the best, Alfred...' he turned and shook hands with Tolley as well: 'You too, Jim. Thank you both for all your hard work. Now I must get back to my office!' He left them with a last wave of the hand.

Chapter Twelve

'Yeh knows yer way ter Northampton Gas?' Tolley asked; Alf shook his head:

'Nah - Oi've been down the Junction a coupl'a toimes but not down that h'arm. Where is it?'

'Yeh goes down the h'arm ter Northampton river, then at the bottom yeh goes straight across inter a little stretch what goes round the back o' Phipps's brew'ry. Gas works is oop there, yeh'll see it. T'ain't far, two 'undred yards mebbe.'

'Roight - thanks Jim. We'll get there!'

Tolley left them after a few more minutes of idle boating chat to go and chase down his replacement horse, eager to get back to work. Mary turned to her husband:

'Yeh've decoided ter let the girls go, 'ave yeh?' Alf shrugged:

'They're both dead set on this h'oidea o' doin' soomat fer the war, love. An' Oi s'pose they're roight, in a way - everyone as can ortta be doin' soomat ter 'elp. What we does is needed, fer what they makes out o' the tar, but Jan's roight when she says as we can manage without the two o' them. Where are they?'

'They'll be back any toime. Suey an' Emmie are off playing wi' Jim's kiddies over there' she waved to a group of children across the yard: 'An' 'Arold's givin' the brasses in ar cabin a quick go.'

'H'okay - once the girls are back we'll get goin', drop ar boat off an get ar stuff moved inter the *Tiber*.'

'Oi've got most of it sorted out ready, Alf, won' take oos long ter move.'

'Tha's good love.'

Minutes later the two older girls returned, shopping bags weighed down with provisions for the next trip. They went to pass them to their mother but Alf intervened:

'Put the stuff away in your boat, it'll save movin' it later.'

'Oh - yeah, roight Pa.' Vera took both bags and descended into the cabin of the *Avon;* Janet gave her father a hopeful look:

'Pa - 'ave yeh thought 'bout what Oi said?'

'Jan - Oi'm still thinkin'. 'Elp oos get these boats ter Saltley, roight?'

'Oh Pa..!' He held up his hand, a warning look on his weather-beaten face, and she subsided. On the boats, the captain held total authority - that was how it had always been. In a working environment that could be, often was, dangerous, one person had to be unquestionably in charge - that was how Janet and her siblings had grown up. But he gave her a smile:

'Let's see 'ow things lie once we're there, eh?'

'H'all roight, Pa.' She gave in gracefully.

'Suey - Emmie! 'Ere now, we're away!' His raised voice echoed across the yard, and the two girls came running.

In the bright, cold afternoon they shafted the two boats back under Stone Street Bridge, under the lattice girder towpath bridge at the junction of the Titford Branch and turned them there where space permitted. That busy co-operation concluded, they settled down for the short journey back along the Birmingham Canal summit, down the three locks at Smethwick and so to the top of the 'Old Thirteen', the flight at the city's end of the Birmingham & Fazeley Canal.

Harold had emerged from the cabin to help with the turn; now he settled in the well of the *Dee* beside his father, looking ahead to where his mother walked behind the mule, keeping it on the move in these unfamiliar surroundings.

'Pa?'

''Arold?'

'Is that roight, we're goin' ter Northampton?'

'S'roight. We'll be on the tar from the gas there ter 'ere, ter Springfield.'

'Oh. Won' be seein' much o' Camplin's then, Oi s'pose?' Alf looked at his son:

'Mebbe not. Oi s'pose they're still on the coal ter the Coventry fact'ries, so we won' be passin' 'em anywhere.' He felt the disappointment radiating from the boy, and spoke again softly: 'We ain't seen 'em fer a whoile any'ow, 'ave we?'

'No, Pa.'

74

They worked down the Thirteen; dusk was falling as they went on down the Six of Ashted, and full dark had descended by the time they reached Bordesley Junction where a left-hand turn led down another five locks of 'The Garrison' to the Fellows, Morton & Clayton yard at Saltley. They left the *Avon* at the junction, tied on the towpath; Alf left his wife to start cooking a meal for them all and took Harold and the two older girls with him to the dock. There, he left them getting the bags and boxes of clothes and kit together and went to find the yard foreman; he'd spotted the *Tiber* already, tied on the towpath opposite, but he needed to let the authorities of the dock know that they had arrived to take it away, and hand over the *Dee* into their care for its docking.

Once again, he was quickly back to the boat, accompanied by the yard manager this time. Joe Barrett was not best pleased, it was past knocking-off time and he'd had to hang around to meet the boatman; but the delay had only been about half an hour, and Kain's cheerful attitude had rubbed off on him as they spoke, walking across to the bank where Harold and the girls waited.

''Arold, Jan, Vera - this is mister Barrett, 'e's' the boss 'ere.' Barrett nodded to them:

'Harold, girls, nice to meet you. Will yeh leave the boat over there where we put your new one, we'll bring it across when we're ready to dock it?'

'O' course, mister Barrett. We'll be back ter the junction ternoight, Oi've left the missus there cookin'. Won' take oos long ter move ar stuff over.'

'And I've got a message for you - from mister Clayton. 'E says can you drop the girls at the BSA fact'ry down Digbeth in the mornin'? They've got jobs for 'em. That's you two, is it?' He asked Janet and Vera; they looked at each other, delighted:

'Yes 'tis, mister Barrett! Thank yeh!' Janet spoke for them both.

'Yeh've got more crew, have yeh mister Kain?' Barrett asked; Alf nodded:

'Oh yeah - there's 'Arold 'ere an' the missus, an' Oi've got two more girls, young'uns. We've been mob-'anded fer a whoile, an' these two reckon as they ortta be doin' soomat fer the war, yeh see.'

'Oh, right. 'Ow old are you, Harold?'

'Fifteen, mister Barrett.' Barrett nodded:

'Too young to be joinin' up then, eh? An' what you're doin' 'elps the war anyway, doesn't it?' He shook hands with Alf: 'Good luck to you all! I'm off 'ome for me dinner.'

'Thanks fer waitin' fer oos, mister Barrett.'

The manager strode away; both girls turned and gave their father a cheerful hug:

'You fixed that, didn' yeh Pa?' Vera asked; Alf nodded:

'Well, yeh both was so keen ter go. Oi asked mister Thomas ter see if there were any jobs goin' as would suit yeh; seems loike there was.'

'Oh, Pa!' Janet gave him a kiss: 'Thank yeh! We'll be seein' yeh from toime ter toime, Oi'm sure?'

'We can come this way on the Northampton trip - we'll stop an' see yeh sometoimes, o' course.' He looked into their faces: 'Coom on, let's get ar stuff shifted an' back ter the *h'Avon* fer ar dinner!'

They poled the *Dee* across the canal, tying it stern-to-stern with the *Tiber,* and set about moving everything that Mary had left ready: Their clothing, bedding and personal things; all the brasses and decorative plates from the cabin, the lace and curtains, their pots and pans, cutlery and crockery. Most of the spare ropes, their water cans and other boating equipment they'd already transferred to the *Avon* during the journey from Oldbury; they could be redistributed later. They worked with a will, and soon were ready to depart; Alf stood for a moment, his arm around his son's shoulders, beside the *Dee:*

'It's been a good boat, eh Dad?' Harold asked.

'S'roight boy. Been ar 'ome for what, foive year? Still, we 'as ter move on - this'un'll do us joost as well, Oi'm sure.' He waved a hand at the *Tiber.* Harold nodded:

'Yeah - it'll soon be 'ome, eh?' Alf laughed:

'Not fer you, boy!'

'What?' Harold was startled; his father laughed:

'If Jan an' Vera are off on the bank fer a whoile, yeh'll be in charge o' th'other boat. It'll be you an' Suey an' Emmie, roight?'

'Oh! Yeah, roight...' Harold took this in.

'Yer Mam'll sort out the sleepin'; but it makes sense if yeh 'ave that'un fer the three o' yeh.'

'Oi s'pose so...' Harold sounded both doubtful and eager at his sudden promotion.

Another hour saw them back at Bordesley Junction, the new boat tied next to the *Avon,* and enjoying a late but delicious stew and jacket potatoes. The enthusiastic discussion centred on Janet and Vera, speculating about the jobs that Thomas Clayton had found for them, and where they might live; but in the absence of definite information it all remained as speculation. Mary gave the *Tiber* a quick examination, grunting her grudging approval of their new home:

. 'Oi'll 'ave ter get the 'angin'-oop plates done roight, an' the laces oop. Mebbe it'll feel loike 'ome then...' Her decorations were presently piled in a box on the floor.

And before she would allow her husband and son to go to bed that night, she had sorted out and put away many of the things that were contained in those boxes, issuing her instructions as she did so:

''Arold - after ternoight, yeh'll be sleepin' in th'other boat, roight? We'll take the girls back ter Digbeth, ter the fact'ry - we'll 'ave ter make sure as they've got somewhere ter stay, Pa? An' make sure they've got their things ter take wi' them.' Alf knew better than to do anything other than grunt his agreement. She went on, half talking to herself:

'Oi wonder if they've 'ad the sense ter sort their stuff out? Oh well, they can do it in the mornin' Oi s'pose. Leave a bit more room fer the kids' clothes - mebbe we can get both of 'em a new steppin' out dress, eh Pa? They're growin' out o' the ones they got... 'Arold - you better sleep on the soide-bed, eh? Yeh can manage h'okay there, leave the cross-bed fer the two girls, now they're gettin bigger...'

At last she was, if not satisfied, at least ready to give it a rest until the morning:

'Oh well - that'll 'ave ter do fer now.' She surveyed her new domain, rubbing her hands together; Harold and his father exchanged looks of grateful relief:

'Can oos get ter bed now then, Missus?' She turned a beaming smile on Alf:

'O' course, Dear!'

Chapter Thirteen

The next morning saw the family parted for the first time in their lives. Mary's goodbye to her two oldest girls as they set off on foot with their father was more painful than she allowed herself to show, holding back her feelings until they were well out of sight; but then her tearful cuddle with Suey and Emmie in the cabin of the *Avon* had Harold feeling sorrowfully useless as he stood by, himself already missing the steady, reliable presence of his sisters. And his new responsibility as skipper of that boat was weighing on his mind a little - he would still be under his father's captaincy, working with him, but now he would have charge of the little details - making sure the boat was clean and smart, that the hatches were properly sealed and secured after loading, that they had all the equipment like ropes and windlasses that they needed, and so on. And keeping his two younger sisters in order..!

They were both sensible, reliable kids - twelve and ten years old, experienced and skilful with both the boat and the mule; and with their liquid cargoes, none of them had to cope with the heavy work of shovelling coal or humping boxes or sacks of other goods when it came to loading or unloading. Thinking of such cargoes reminded him of the Camplings and their work on the Coventry Canal, and that he wouldn't have the chance to run into Annie for the foreseeable future. He felt a surge of regret well up inside him. He was fifteen, approaching sixteen; Annie would be what, just turned fifteen? Too young, either of them, for him to be thinking of really courting - but now it seemed as if that opportunity was going to be denied him anyway...

The factory of the Birmingham Small Arms company was situated beside Digbeth Basin, once the terminus at the end of a branch of the Birmingham & Fazeley Canal. The junction where they had spent the night was barely two hundred yards from where the later Grand Junction Canal had joined the Birmingham system over a hundred years ago, linking the midland industries with London via the River Thames at

Brentford; it took Alf and the girls only a quarter of an hour to make their way there and find their way to the factory gates. The shift manager, a tall, dark-haired young man, came out to meet them, shaking hands all round:

'Oh yes, we're taking on more and more girls to work here, mister Kain' he assured Alf in response to his question: 'So many of our young men have left to join the army, we'd be struggling to keep up without them!'

'Can yeh foind ar girls somewhere ter stay? We live in the boat, yeh see.'

'Oh yes, don't worry about that! We knew your situation, and the boss has got digs lined up for you. Not far away, with a family who work here themselves - their sons are away in France, and they're happy to take you in' he addressed Janet and Vera: 'Do you have your personal things with you?'

'No sir' Janet told him: 'Moy Pa'll bring them along; we didn' know where we moight be goin', yeh see.'

'Call me mister Grant! I'm just a shift boss. How old are you both?'

'Oi'm twenny, twenny-one in January; Vera's eighteen.'

'That's fine - do you want to start straight away?' They looked at each other and nodded:

'Yes, mister Grant. If someone can show oos what ter do!'

'All right - come with me. Mister Kain - if you want to bring their clothes to the office here I'll see that they're taken around to Fred Freeman's house.'

'Thank yeh, mister Grant, Oi'll pop 'em along roight away, then we'll 'ave ter get goin'.' He turned to the girls: 'Jan; Vera...' They grabbed him into a tight three-way hug:

'Take care, Pa.'

'Oi will Jan - you too eh?'

'Love yeh, Pa.'

'Love you too Vera; both o' yeh. We'll be by ter see yeh soon, eh?'

'Yes Pa...'

He found himself having to brush away a tear as he walked back to the boats.

The girls had left their personal things ready, packed into a couple of old boxes; Harold helped his father carry them to the factory where they left them with a sympathetic lady in the front office. Back at the boats, they found that Mary and the two smaller girls had moved Harold's things into the *Avon* and finished putting the cabin of the *Tiber* in order, if not entirely to Mary's liking at least to something she would accept 'for now'. The mules had spent their night grazing on the towpath for once; Suey and Emmie had filled their time while their sisters departed by giving them a really good grooming and making a big fuss of them, feeding them oats in handfuls; when Harold and his father returned, they were ready to set off.

The journey in front of them comprised fifty miles and ninety-two locks, three days travel given that they didn't know 'the road'. Leaving Bordesley on the Thursday morning, they in fact took their time, knowing that they wouldn't reach Northampton in time to be loaded before the weekend. Following the boaters' 'middle road' up Camp Hill locks onto the ten-mile pound then down the five at Knowle, they finished the day after running down the twenty-one of Hatton after dark, tying just above Cape Two in Warwick. They joined a number of other boats there opposite the Cape of Good Hope, where Alf and Mary headed for a glass of ale, leaving Harold to see his two little sisters settled for the night after taking the ponies to the pub stables, before joining them. Their mood was subdued, despite the presence in the pub of a number of other boaters, each of them feeling the absence of the older girls.

Inevitably, the general conversation drifted into talk of the war. The end of 1915, almost a year and a half of fighting, and the conflict seemed to be going nowhere. In the middle east, the failed invasion of Gallipoli had collapsed and the British and Commonwealth forces had been evacuated; the fighting in Mesopotamia had ground to halt south of Baghdad. In eastern Europe, Serbia was all-but defeated, her army in full retreat into Albania; the Italian offensive against the Austro-Hungarians had also reached a stalemate as the winter weather closed in. On the eastern front, there too the fighting had stagnated as heavy rains turned the roads into quagmires and any movement of forces became impossible; in the west, in the Champagne region, British and French forces had pushed the Germans back but the gains were relatively small, and again bad weather had brought things to a halt.

At sea, German U-boats continued to sink shipping indiscriminately to a growing level of protest from the US government; and nearer to home for the boaters gathered that night were the increasing raids on English cities by the Zeppelins. Aeroplanes were coming into increasing use as their technology developed under the pressure of the need to intercept such raids as well as to provide artillery spotting and air-cover for the fighting in France and elsewhere.

Friday saw them away from Warwick and through Leamington Spa, where they had loaded on the way north; across the Avon Valley and then uphill through the Fosse locks, through Bascote Four with its two-lock staircase; up the flight at Stockton and the three at Calcutt and so onto a stretch of the Oxford Canal which was unfamiliar territory for them, turning east towards Braunston. Now on the Grand Junction Canal, they were up the six Braunston locks it seemed in no time, the wide chambers here allowing both boats in at once; then through the tunnel and across the short summit for a relatively early stop at the top of Buckby Locks, outside the New Inn.

The day had seen them all settling into a new routine, working the two boats with just the five of them. Susan and Emily found themselves working harder than they were used to, with all the same tasks having to be covered by fewer people, but they set to with a will, challenged by Harold to prove that they could work the boats along just as quickly without Janet and Vera. At the pub, Alf took the two girls along after they'd put the ponies in the stables, treating them to a glass of lemonade each 'now yeh're 'avin' ter be growed-oop'.

Saturday, and a quick run down the seven wide locks of Buckby; twelve miles on the level to Gayton Junction where the arm to Northampton turns off from the Grand Junction main line. Another four and a half miles and they were there - but that distance includes the seventeen locks that drop down to the River Nene. And these are again narrow locks, so they were working each one twice to pass the pair of boats. Emerging from the narrow arm onto the wide river, Alf easily spotted the entrance diagonally opposite, as Jim Tolley had told him, into another narrow arm which led away around the impressive brewery buildings. The girls led their ponies away and across the nearby road bridge to the towpath on the far side of the river; and then, the flow being relatively gentle, Alf and Harold poled the boats over to join them before setting off up the arm to find the gas works. They tied behind the works buildings as dusk was sinking into darkness.

Sunday was spent cleaning the boats, Mary fussing over getting the cabin of the *Tiber* just the way she wanted it. In the afternoon, they took an expedition into the town to find the local shops and public baths, where all enjoyed a good soak and scrub after their long trip. Monday morning came, and they loaded for the first time on their new job, fifty tons of tar residues destined for the Springfield Works back in Oldbury. Soon a new routine established itself - the round trip would take them just a week, three days of travel in each direction, the seventh day used in loading or unloading.

And so Christmas 1915 passed; winter turned into spring, and with the improving weather the fighting across Europe and around the world resumed...

Chapter Fourteen

As Alfred had surmised, during this time both Campling brothers had spent their working lives on the delivery of coal from the Warwickshire coalfields to the factories of Coventry, their work subcontracted from the Samuel Barlow Coal Company Limited. Coventry's motor industry had been turned over to war production, so their work was very much in support of the military; but Jacob remained uncomfortable with his role, fretting that he was still at sixteen too young to volunteer 'officially'. They were all aware of other boys, his age and even younger, who had succeeded in joining up, pulling the wool over the eyes of the recruiting officers - the death of his friend Jackie had hit him hard, but in an odd way served at the same time to reinforce his feeling that he too should be doing more. And an incident that summer was to unsettle him even further...

Robert Carson was an angry, bitter man. In his late fifties, he'd served in the army for many years and fought in the Boer War; retired in 1906, he'd become a policeman in Coventry, his home town. When war was declared in 1914, he'd tried to sign up but been rejected as too old; but they'd taken his son Richard, the pride of his life. His pride had survived into 1915 - until they received the telegram from the War Office. Part of his bitterness arose from a feeling that it should have been him, the experienced ex-lance-corporal, who had died in a hail of bullets on the Bellewaarde Ridge.

One of his daughters was a nurse, serving behind the western front, and her letters did nothing to ease his pain even if she tried her best to disguise the terrible loss of life that was going on there; his youngest had given up her studies to work in the Alvis car factory, now making vehicles for the army. Although he recognised that his own job was of value, nevertheless his frustration left him continually on the verge of anger that could become incandescent at times; only his wife's calm acceptance of their lot in life and young Eileen's talk of the future, of going back to college once the war was over and taking up her career as a teacher, kept him from a spiral of pain and fury.

Robert enjoyed a pint of bitter, and the conversation of a regular group of factory workers he'd often meet in the Longford Engine on his way home after his afternoon shifts. No-one worried about his uniform; he'd keep his helmet tucked under his arm to signify his off-duty status as he quaffed a pint or two, discussing the progress of the war and criticising its conduct as ex-soldiers will always do.

A warm Thursday evening in early June, and he leant on a corner of the bar with two of his drinking mates; the clock ticked its way around to nine o'clock.

Two couples came in together and walked up to the bar:

'What yeh 'avin' Seph?' Josiah Campling asked his brother.

'Pint o' moild please, Siah, an' a stout fer Beth.'

'Stout fer you too, Joan?' His wife nodded, and the landlord began to serve them, drawing two pints before turning to his shelves for the bottles of stout. Josiah settled up and pocketed his change:

'Makes a change, stoppin' 'ere, eh Seph?'

'Yeah. Whoy they won' let yeh stay in the basin Oi've never known! An' the Grey'ound'd be crowded by the toime we got there ternoight, eh?'

'S'roight. Oi didn' fancy a big crowd ternoight - 'ope yeh don' moind?'

'Nah - gi's the chance ter talk, eh?'

'Yeah... Listen, Seph - Oi knows what we're doin' wi' the coal ter the fact'ries is h'important, but... They was askin' fer boats ter go on the run from Birnigum ter Lunnon, ter take guns an' h'ammunition ter the docks - 'ad yeh 'eard?'

'Yeah. Yeh thinkin' o' goin' fer it?'

'Mebbe. They're payin' h'extra.'

'An' it would suit ar Jake better! 'E's still goin' on 'bout joinin' oop, but Oi don' want 'im ter.'

Beside them, the women were having their own conversation:

'How's your Johnnie doin'?' Joan was asking.

''E's foine - we got a message from Grannie Camplin' th'other day. 'E's mooch better, got rid o' that awful cough now.'

'Are you havin' him back on the boat then?' But Beth shook her head:

'Not yet. 'E's doin' well in school, she reckons...' She glanced at her husband and leant close, speaking softly: 'Oi knows Seph don' put mooch store by it, but Oi reckon a bit o' learnin'll do 'im good later in loife. Won' do 'im no 'arm, any'ow. So Oi'm leavin' 'im there fer now. Oi ain't told Seph 'ow mooch better 'e is, an' Grannie ain't lettin' on neither! We'll fetch 'im back in toime.' They shared a smile; as a 'scholard' off the bank, Joan's sympathies were with her:

'How old is Annie now? She's getting to be a really pretty girl, isn't she?' Beth smiled proudly:

'Aye, she is, ain't she? She's fifteen, sixteen in November.'

'Not got a boyfriend yet?'

'Ah, well - she were a bit keen on young 'Arold Kain, but we ain't seen 'em fer a whoile. Someone said as they're workin' Northampton ter h'Oldb'ry now.'

'Oh, that's a pity, he's a nice lad.'

The door opened to admit Jacob and Ann, returned from feeding and grooming the ponies in the pub stables. Joseph turned to the landlord:

'Can we 'ave a pint o' shandy an' a lemonade please mate?' Jacob went to join the men, Annie to her mother's side; in the other corner of the room, Robert Carson had looked up as they came in. Now he gazed at Jacob, a frown on his face, as the boy took the proffered glass; he stood up slowly, leaving his companions, and walked across to the boaters. They turned to him as he approached:

'Evenin', h'Officer' Siah spoke to him, but his eyes were on Jacob:

'What are you doing here? Why aren't you fighting for your country? Haven't you heard, all young men are expected to join the armed services! Everyone from eighteen to forty is liable for service now!'

Jake stared at him, taken aback and lost for words; his father took a step forward, his anger clear on his face:

''E ain't even seventeen yet, never moind eighteen! You leave oos alone, we're doin' ar bit!'

'What we does keeps the fact'ries goin'.' Josiah added: 'If we didn' do what we do, your precious soldiers wouldn' 'ave no guns nor bullets nor wagons nor nothin'!'

'He's old enough to carry a gun!' Carson retorted: 'If he isn't eighteen, how come you're buying him alcohol?' Joseph and Josiah exchanged guilty looks, but Siah came back:

'We been on the go since six this mornin'! Oi reckon as 'e's' earnt a bit o' consideration, even from the loikes o' you!'

'Leave it, Bob' the landlord intervened: 'You ain't on duty now - let the boy have his refreshment.' Carson glared at him, but he backed down and stalked back to his friends, grumbling under his breath. The landlord turned to the boaters:

'Bob's a bit touchy, he lost his boy in France last year, at Ypres. But he's right - I shouldn't sell you beer for your lad if he's really that young? You look older, boy!' he told Jake with a smile: 'That's my excuse, anyway!'

'Thanks, mate' Seph relaxed. He looked at the watch in his waistcoat pocket: 'Better drink oop any'ow, we needs ter be away in the mornin', get ter Sutton's an' join the queue fer h'orders.' His brother nodded:

'Aye. Coom on, get it down yeh!'

They all drained their glasses and headed for the door, but after a moment's pause Jacob turned back. He went over to the little group in the corner:

'H'excuse me - sir, Oi'm really sorry, about what 'appened ter your son. Oi do want ter do me bit, when Oi'm older; an' what moy Ooncle says is roight, we're doin' what we're able ter, even now.'

Carson gazed at him for a moment, and Jake was astonished to see the glitter of tears in the man's eyes. Then he held out his hand:

'Thank you, son. I - I thought you were older. I... I spoke out of turn; I'm sorry if I upset you.' Jake shook his hand:

'That's h'all roight.' Carson nodded; they parted and Jake hurried to catch up with his family. Annie, seeing him slip back, had paused to wait for him; as he caught up with her she slipped her arm through his with a smile.

Back at the boats, the brothers stood talking on the towpath while their wives arranged the beds in their cabins:

'What d'yeh reckon ter this other job, Siah?'

'The guns an' stuff? Oi ain't sure, Seph. Money's better, an' they say as there'd be back-loads, groceries an' the loike. Could be good, eh?' Jake came and joined them as Annie ducked into her cabin to get ready for bed:

'What's it all about, Pa?'

'The coomp'ny's lookin' fer boats ter carry moonitions ter Lunnon. An' back wi' groceries.'

'Oh? Sounds good ter me! More money, an' we 'd really be doin' soomat fer the war, wouldn' we? Yeh goin' ter take it?'

'Oi dunno, Jake. Oi don' loike the h'oidea o' cargoes that could h'explode on oos - look what 'appened las' toime at Blow-Up Bridge!' Macclesfield Bridge on the Regent's Canal had been completely destroyed during the Napoleonic wars when a boat laden with gunpowder had blown up directly under the massive masonry structure, killing its crew and a number of passers-by.

'Things 'ave changed since then, Seph - they packs the stuff better ter keep it safe nowadays.' Siah reminded him.

'Oi still ain't 'appy, Siah. The money sounds good, all roight, but... Oi dunno. An' we got a decent steady job now, ain't we?'

'Let's think about it, Pa?' Jake encouraged him; his father hesitated:

'H'okay, Oi'll think 'bout it! 'Appy?'

'A'roight Pa!' Jake knew when not to push his father.

They were at Sutton's Stop by 7am the next day. Boats were beginning to depart, heading for the most part to the various collieries to load, while other boatmen were congregating, awaiting their turn to be called to the office for their orders. The brothers joined a small knot of them, outside the Greyhound public house, where the war was the inevitable subject of discussion. Jim Nixon, as ever, was holding forth:

'Well, Oi don' reckon as 'e were doin' such a great job. Oi mean, we should'a 'ad 'em beat ages ago!'

''Oo yeh talkin' about?' Josiah asked as they strolled up; Nixon turned to him:

'Lord Kitchener! Ain't you 'eard?'

''Eard what?'

''E got killed, th'other day.'

''Is ship got sunk' another boater informed them: 'On their way ter Roossia, they was.'

'That roight? Bugger!'

Lord Kitchener had been the Secretary for War in the government, a man whose face was familiar to all from the famous recruiting posters - "Your Country Needs You!"; he'd gone down in the North Sea with HMS Hampshire. The argument about his conduct of the war moved on to talk of the latest developments, of the Battle of Jutland, off the coast of Denmark, where the Royal Navy had driven the German High Seas Fleet back to their bases after an attempted sortie into the North Sea; despite losing a number of important ships it was being claimed as a major victory in the press. Of the fighting in Europe, the men, lacking a knowledge of the geography, felt an ongoing, frustrating degree of confusion as news of battles, of gains and losses, left them unable to understand the overall trends: 'So 'oo's winnin'?' was a frequent query.

One thing they could understand was the reports of the growing anger in America towards the German offensive at sea, the number of US citizens killed aboard the ships sunk by U-boats:

'They'll be joinin' in soon, on ar soide, you mark moy words!' was Nixon's view of the matter.

'What's all this 'bout 'em lookin' fer boats to go on the moonitions runs?' Joseph changed the subject.

'Yeah, s'roight. Some goes by train but they reckon as it's safer on the boats, so they're askin' fer men ter tek it on' Nixon confirmed. Jacob had stood to one side, just listening in until now:

'What d'yeh reckon, Pa?'

'Dunno, boy! You goin' fer it, Jim?' Nixon shook his head:

'Oi'm wi' Barlows, Oi does what Oi'm told. But yeh're noomber ones, the two o' yeh, yeh can do as yeh loikes.'

'Pa..?'

'Oi'm thinkin', boy!'

Chapter Fifteen

So 1916, the second full year of war, slipped by. Against the background of the widespread, ongoing conflict, life and work on the boats went on much as ever even if many boats were now engaged upon trips that directly supported the war effort - carrying not only munitions but raw materials and fuel for the factories, and foodstuffs to keep the working population healthy and happy. Narrowboats were even employed to carry battalions of soldiers crammed into the open holds from their training camps to the docks to go and join the fighting.

More and more of the young men from boating families disappeared, some voluntarily, others conscripted since the law allowing it had been passed early in the year. Transport was seen as a reserved occupation, and many of them could if they'd chosen have avoided the call-up - if they had been able to read and fill in the forms needed to register their protected status.

War news, as always, spread among the boaters by word of mouth, 'scholards' like Joan Campling picking up and reading out newspapers, better-informed wharf and dock hands or pub landlords contributing to the dissemination of information. So they came to know of the intense fighting in France and Belgium, of the German offensive around Verdun and the Allied counter-attacks in the Somme region; some amazement was raised by the first appearance of strange, heavily-armoured fighting machines referred to as 'tanks'. And snippets of the other theatres of war, in the Balkans, in the Middle East, in Russia and Poland, which meant little to them except for the way they influenced the overall balance of the conflict. Of more import were the events closer to home: The German High Seas Fleet being once again blocked from its sorties into the North Sea by the Royal Navy; more raids over London and other areas by Zeppelin airships, the shooting down of a few of them raising a cheer; and disgust at the report of the first air raids on England by German bomber aeroplanes.

The biggest news in Britain through that autumn was the horrendous lists of casualties published almost daily from the seemingly-endless battle of the Somme, a major British offensive that failed to break the German lines and descended into months of almost aimless back-and-forth fighting. There was a growing sense of futility among those at home as so many young men were wounded or killed for no obvious useful purpose.

***

A cold, drizzly Saturday in September, and Alfred Kain's mood was one of tightly-controlled fury. Fury with his son, who stood before him, head down, looking and feeling very sheepish and stupid, aware that he fully deserved the haranguing he was receiving; the grey and dismal weather wasn't helping his father's mood, but he knew and accepted that he was responsible for most of it.

The Northampton Arm of the Grand Junction Canal turns off from the main London-to-Birmingham route, which passes along a sixteen-mile level pound across Northamptonshire between Whilton and Stoke Bruerne, passing the town of Weedon and the villages of Bugbrooke, Gayton and Blisworth on its way. Gayton Junction lies to the north of the long darkness of Blisworth Tunnel; the Arm then stretches for four and a half miles to its confluence with the older navigation of the River Nene, close to South Bridge in Northampton. But in that short distance it falls through almost a hundred feet into the river valley, much of that descent occurring through the impressive flight of thirteen Rothersthorpe locks, a mile of continuous effort for the crew of a pair of boats. Thence they have a short break, a half-mile pound to the next lock, and then the ground levels out, only three further locks in over two miles finally dropping the boats into the river.

It was after the energy-sapping work of 'The Thick', on the length to Wootton Lock, that Harold had allowed his mind to wander. They had been on this same run for nine months now, and knew every twist and turn of the road, its changing moods with the changing weather, and in such circumstances complacency can creep in almost unnoticed. And the news from France was in his mind; news that upset him, and made him think about all the effort that was going into the war, and the fear that it was all for nothing. And thinking of all that effort, at home as well as in the trenches, made him think of those he knew who were involved - his two sisters, working in the armaments factory in Birmingham - and friends who were carrying those weapons to the docks...

He hadn't seen Annie Campling for more than a year. As he'd helped work his parents' boat through Wootton Lock, half of his mind had been occupied with the image of her pretty round face, her sparkling dark eyes and appealing smile, with questions about where she was, what she might be doing... Who she might be with...

Alf had brought the *Tiber* to halt beneath Banbury Lane Bridge, immediately below the lock, and come back to help with the *Avon*. Buddy drew the empty boat into the refilled lock; Emmie swung the top gate closed as he and Harold whipped up the bottom paddles, but as he'd gone to return to his boat and set off towards Hardingstone Lock a shout from Suey, at the tiller of the *Avon*, had stopped him in his tracks:

''Arold! 'Ellum's on the cill!' A moment of careless inattention, and the boat had drifted back as it sank in the lock until the massive wooden rudder had come down onto the top of what was in effect the threshold of the upper gate. By the time they could drop the paddles and stop its descent it was too late - the rudder, hung on two hook-like pintles to the stern of the boat, had lifted off and fallen sideways. Restrained by a length of chain which was there for just such incidents, it remained attached to the boat but no longer sitting in its pivots.

''Arold?'

'Pa...'

'What was yeh thinkin' 'bout, boy?'

'Dunno, Pa...' It was his responsibility to make sure that errors like this didn't happen, to loop a rope over the lockside bollard to hold the boat forward, and he'd failed. Distracted by his thoughts, he'd relied on the flow of water from the lock to

93

hold it in place, and hadn't noticed its slow drift backwards; and now they faced the arduous task of relocating the rudder on its pintles. The weight of the rudder was such that one man could barely lift it never mind manoeuvre it back into place; and the lower pintle was out of sight below the water, making that manoeuvring even more difficult. And so it was that Harold stood there, eyes averted, as his father expressed his displeasure in terms forceful enough to make his two youngest daughters snigger even as they blushed.

Half an hour later, Alf was standing precariously on the tiny triangular stern deck, a rope looped several times over his shoulders and passing through a hole in the rudder, straining his back to support its weight while Harold, standing on the cill in the bottom of the now-empty lock, pushed and heaved to line the two hooks on the rudder up with the pintles on the stern-post of the boat. They had tried a number of times already, but each time that Alf had had to lower the rudder and rest his back one or the other of the hooks had missed their targets, to his ever-growing annoyance and Harold's similarly growing embarrassment.

One more try - Alf braced himself, straightening his back and heaving the rudder up; Harold pushed it carefully sideways so that the hooks hovered over their receptacles:

''Kay Pa!' He concentrated on guiding the lower hook to the pintle he could barely make out through the cloudy water; Alf kept the rudder steady, the upper hook over its socket at the peak of the deck between his feet, and eased it gently down. And at last it settled into its assigned place, the hooks engaging with their pintles, swinging freely when Harold gave it a trial push to the side. He stood back and looked up at his father; Alf slipped the rope from his shoulders and stretched his back. His anger had abated, but the lost time and the effort expended to put right his son's carelessness still rankled; he looked down at Harold with a grim smile:

'Yeh ain't gonna do that agen in a 'urry, are yeh boy?'

'No, Pa. Oi'm sorry, Oi wasn' watchin' what Oi was at.'

94

'That yeh wasn', boy. Yeh ortta know better, yeh're a better boater'n that.'

'Oi know, Pa.' Alf gazed into his son's eyes:

'Annie Camplin'?' Harold essayed a thin smile and nodded; his father's smile grew wider: 'Oi moight'a guessed! Yeh really miss seein' 'er, don' yeh lad?' Harold nodded again:

'Yeah...' Alf reached out and took his arm, helping him over into the stern well of the boat:

'Oi knows what its loike, 'Arold. Oi was yer age once!'

'Thanks Pa. Oi won' let yeh down agen.'

'Oi knows that boy. An' we'll come across Camplin's agen sooner or later - if it's meant ter be, it'll 'appen, roight?'

'Yes, Pa.' Alf slipped an arm around his son's shoulders and gave them a quick squeeze before jumping onto the cabin roof and thence up onto the lockside:

'Coom on, we gotta get goin'!'

Chapter Sixteen

Autumn slipped into winter; the news from abroad hardly improved although as the fighting on the Somme and around Verdun ground to its usual winter-time stalemate the casualty lists correspondingly decreased. Britain saw a new Prime Minister when Herbert Asquith resigned to be replaced by David Lloyd-George, and the political mood in Russia took another dramatic turn when the Tsarina's favourite, the monk Rasputin, was murdered by disaffected elements.

On board the *Alice Rose,* Joseph's conservatism still ruled. Despite, or even maybe because of, the constant gentle hints dropped by Jacob, he clung to the job they knew and understood, running coal from the collieries of Warwickshire to the basin in Coventry for distribution to the many and varied factories of the city with an occasional trip to Birmingham instead to supply the military production there. Even when his older brother opted for the more lucrative munitions trade at the beginning of September, he clung to the familiar and reliable.

Jacob, beneath his calm, cheerful exterior, was still torn between his desire to be more directly active in the war and his respect for his father's wishes. He knew that much of Joseph's reluctance to let him sign up for the army was down to the fear that he would die or be seriously injured; and the loss of Jackie Barnet still caused him a deep sadness at the same time as making him feel guilty that he was staying safe at home. They both knew that other young men like Jackie had been accepted despite being under-age, but Joseph had dug his heels in:

'If yeh troies it we'll tell 'em yer real age, boy! Mebbe when yeh're eighteen...' with his fingers firmly crossed that the fighting would be over by then.

Johnnie had stayed with his grandmother - his parents would get occasional messages through the traffic office at Sutton's, telling them of his progress, and Joseph would sometimes express his wish to have his younger son with him again. A wish that would be deflected by his wife, reminding him that the boy was there for the sake of his health while carefully neglecting to tell him how much recovered he was...

Ann, at sixteen, had grown into an attractive young woman; not tall, as was usual among the boaters, but slim and pretty with her thick dark hair and warm brown eyes. She had been amused recently to be the centre of attention sometimes when they stopped overnight, especially while they awaited orders at Hawkesbury, among the boating youth, the teenage boys surreptitiously competing to talk to her. There were those she liked, one or two she found quite attractive in their own way; but at times she would still hold in her mind the image of the tall blond-haired boy on the Clayton boats, and wonder where he was, what he might be doing, and feel a pang of jealousy if she imagined him with other girls...

Christmas Eve, and the object of her thoughts was standing in a corner of the bar of the Prince of Wales, above Old Turn Junction in central Birmingham. Popular with the boaters, a good number had gathered there for the holiday, and in the smoky atmosphere considerable volumes of mild and bitter ale were being consumed, many glasses of stout and not a small amount of lemonade among the younger elements.

The mix of families from the boats moored below at Cambrian Wharf and around the junction were having a riotous evening; the big bar had been partly cleared and couples were step-dancing in the middle of the room to music from melodeons and banjoes. All ages were there, children gathered in one corner talking and playing together, the men talking shop or discussing the war, the women comparing family matters. A group of teenagers chatted together - a much reduced group than it might have been, one of the subjects of conversation those from among their number who were absent in the armed forces. In a few cases that absence had become permanent, and a sense of deep melancholy hung over them for a time before the robustness of youth returned to raise their spirits.

Among them, Harold stood out to any observer - taking after his father, he was taller at sixteen than most of the older boatmen who tended to stockiness, and his thick blond hair seemed to gleam over his companions' heads under the pub's newly-fitted electric lights. Eyes scanning the crowd from the street door just after nine o'clock easily picked him out; he turned as a hand gripped his shoulder, to look into his sister's eyes:

'Jan! Oh, it's grand ter see yeh!' He flung his arms around her neck and she hugged him tightly:

''Arold! 'Ow are yeh, little brother?' Releasing her, he grabbed his other sister into an embrace:

'Vera! 'Ow are yeh doin', both o' yeh?'

'We're foine, 'Arold! Look 'oo we found at Digbeth on ar way 'ere!' He raised his head to see Josiah and Joan Campling grinning at him over her shoulder:

'Mister Camplin'; missus Camplin' - it's good ter see yeh an' all!' Josiah shook his hand:

'We're loadin' at the BSA terday, an' we ran inter yer sisters there a whoile ago, 'Arold; they said as yeh'd be meetin' oop 'ere ternoight. 'Ow are yeh, lad? Yer Mam an' Dad about?'

'Oi'm foine, mister Camplin'; Pa an' Mam are over there somewhere' he waved to the far corner of the room: 'They'll be 'appy ter see yeh!' Siah patted the boy's shoulder:

'We'll go foind 'em. Good ter see yeh, boy!' Joan stretched up to give him a peck on the cheek, and they fought their way through the crowd to where his parents were enjoying the music and frivolity with the other boaters.

Christmas Eve in 'the public' was always a time of pure relaxation and enjoyment, a time when concerns would be put aside and talking shop was strictly forbidden. Even in time of war frivolity was allowed to take over, even if to many there was an undercurrent of disquiet aroused by the absence of friends or loved ones. But partway through the evening the arrival of another crew turned the mood briefly from Major to Minor: About nine o'clock the doors opened to admit a tall, stooped figure familiar to everyone - Arthur Yorke was a Fellows Morton & Clayton captain with a pair of horse-boats. His appearance was greeted with a welcoming chorus as his diminutive wife Doris followed him in; but then a hush descended upon the gathering. Behind them came their eldest son.

Albert Yorke was barely nineteen. He hobbled in, leaning on wooden crutches, his left trouser leg tucked up into his waistband, heavy bandages encircling the left side of his head, covering his eye and cheek. Vera Kain had been rather sweet on Albert in the past; now, she stared at him in suppressed horror:

'Albert...'

What they could see of his mouth stretched into a grin:

'Aye, it's me Vera. 'Ow are yeh?'

'Oi'm h'okay Albert...' The injured lad stepped forward into the room, his siblings crowding behind him but careful not to knock him off-balance; he grinned even wider:

'Oi've 'ad a bit of a problem, meself.'

'So we can see, lad' an anonymous voice rose from the crowd. Another called to the landlord:

'Tommy! Gi's a pint fer Albert, looks loike 'e's earnt it!'

Moments later, a row of glasses stood on the bar:

'Albert, Arthur, Doris - on the 'ouse.' Albert wobbled over; he leant the crutches against the bar, propping himself there too:

'Thank yeh, Tom! Yeh don' 'ave ter, though.' He took a long pull at his pint: 'Ah! Proper beer! That's grand! They wouldn' let me 'ave none in th'orspital.' He looked around at the silent faces: 'Don' look so glum! Oi'm still 'ere. Well, most o' me is any'ow.' After a moment, a nervous voice asked:

'What 'appened, Albert?' The boy grinned again:

'Got caught by a shell-blast, in the trench along from where Oi was. Me mates that soide o' me all bought it, Oi was the nearest one that made it, but it took me leg off, smashed me oop a bit. They saved me arm - just as well, it'd be awkward wi' the crutches else.'

'Oh, Albert...' Vera was on the verge of tears. He reached out, slipped an arm around her shoulders:

'Loike Oi said, Oi'm still 'ere. The ones ter feel sorry fer are them as ain't. Lots of ar lads are dyin' over there, every day.' He raised his voice: 'Mebbe Oi've only got one leg, an'

one eye, but Oi'm aloive, roight? It's Christmas Eve, an' Oi'm
goin' ter celebrate bein' 'ere ter see it! Coom on, join me, all o'
yeh!'

The rest of the evening passed in a sense of subdued joy;
Vera stayed by the wounded boy's side, talking softly with him.
Some families drifted off early to put young children to bed, but
many stayed until midnight or beyond until at last a general
move towards the doors and their warm, comfortable cabins
began.

Waving a goodnight to others they had been talking and
singing with, Alf Kain put a hand on his friend's shoulder:

'D'yeh see mooch o' Seph these days, Siah?'

'Oh aye, we sees 'em every now an' then. Some of ar back-
loads tek oos their way, oop ter Tam'orth or that soide o'
Birnigum so we stops off ter catch 'em at Sutton's.'

'Yeh mostly goes middle-road?'

'S'roight - quickest way from Digbeth's oop Camp 'Ill an'
down by 'Atton. Top road'd be a long way round an' bottom
road's too slow, but loike Oi said we gets that way now an' agen.'

'Ah. Say 'ello ter Seph an' Beth fer oos, eh? Wish 'em well.'
Siah clapped him on the back:

'Oi will, o' course Alf! Oi'm sure they'd say the same ter
you.'

Harold had been listening in to this:

'Mister Camplin'? Would yeh pass on a message fer me
too?' Siah cocked an eye at him:

'Yeah, o' course 'Arold - what is it?'

'Um, well - would yeh say ter Annie that...' He found
himself lost for words; Siah grinned at him:

'Oi'll say as yeh're thinkin' of 'er, shall Oi?'

'Yeah, thanks! An' tell 'er Oi'm 'opin Oi'll see 'er agen some
day soon?'

'Oi will boy!' It was Harold's turn to flinch at the weight of
Siah's friendly slap on his shoulder; the boatman eyed him for a
moment: 'Pretty girl, Ar Annie. Lookin' real growed-oop too
she is, now.'

'Yeah, Oi s'pose she is...' Harold sounded less than happy at this, and Siah's grin grew sympathetic:

'If it's any consolation to yeh, she ain't got a fella, 'Arold. Not as there ain't plenty o' boys as would tek the job!' He turned to Alf: 'Yeh goes top road?' Alf nodded:

'Aye. From Northampton it's oop ter Brarnston, Wigrams an' 'Atton then oop Lap'orth, it's ar quickest road ter h'Ol'bry.'

'So yeh'd be passin' them if they was ter get on the moonitions trip wi' oos, eh?' Siah sounded thoughtful, and Harold nodded eagerly:

'D'yeh reckon as they moight do that?' Siah laughed:

'It'd suit Jake, 'e's been on about it fer ages, reckons they'd be doin' more fer the war that way! An' if Oi mentions it ter Annie, mebbe she'd be after 'er Pa ter do it an' all, eh? Money's better too, as Oi keeps tellin' 'im.'

Nothing more was said; Harold knew not to push the point any more, but the conspiratorial expression on Josiah's face was enough to tell him the older man was on his side and would use his influence with his brother if he could.

Chapter Seventeen

Jacob Campling was cold and wet and heartily fed up with his lot. Tramping along, almost blinded by the icy rain blowing straight into his face in the pitch darkness, he would have taken any offer of a different life, even the mud and depredation that he'd seen in newspaper photographs of the trenches in Flanders; and that niggling feeling that he ought to be doing more for his country was still there, lurking in the back of his mind. But here he was, his heavy overcoat dribbling ice-cold water into his boots, his cap pulled right down over his eyes but still failing to keep the driving rain out of them, having to encourage the reluctant pony along when it too would have given up and stopped where it was given half a chance. He reached out to give it a gentle slap on its rump:

'Good girl, Molly! We'll be ter Sutton's soon, then we can both get warm an' dry, eh?'

The middle of January, 1917; they had loaded that day at Baddesley Colliery basin, halfway down the flight of locks at Atherstone, held up in a queue of boats until mid-afternoon. And then just as they set off for Coventry, their load destined for the wharves there where it would be distributed to whatever factory needed the supply, dusk had brought with it a howling Atlantic storm which had several times almost had them wind-bound in the open countryside above the locks, pinned against the bank and fighting just to keep moving. But come what might his father had insisted on pressing on, intent on reaching the canal junction at Hawkesbury and the welcoming warmth of the Greyhound even if they couldn't make the city basin. They'd battled their way around the twists and turns of the canal, through the town of Nuneaton, past the junction with the Ashby Canal where they would sometimes go to load, and on towards Bedworth. Now, at last, the end was near if not exactly in sight; around the sharp bend opposite Charity Dock, past the back of the town, another turn under Bedworth Hill Bridge by the entrance of the Newdigate Colliery arm and they were on the last easy stretch, a mile to go around gentle bends to the junction, a centre of canal life where empty boats would gather to await their orders and passing loaded boats like themselves would choose to stop for the company of their fellows.

Approaching the junction, he let Molly draw to a halt behind the first of a line of moored boats. His father steered the *Alice Rose* in against the towpath bank and stepped off with the stern line; Jacob held the towline, unhitched from Molly's spreader-bar, its eye still over the looby at the top of the mast, leaning into it to hold the boat tight while Joseph tied the stern and then hurried past him to grab the fore-end line and moor the front. With the boat secured, Jake took Molly by the bridle and led her along the towpath, over the curving iron bridge at the junction and into the stables opposite the pub, stripping off her harness and giving her a quick rub-down, making sure she had plenty of food to hand. And then at last he could head back to the boat to get himself dry.

Scrambling down into the little fore-cabin, he raised a smile when he saw that the pot-bellied stove in there was well alight, almost glowing; either his mother or more probably Annie had been stoking it up for him along the way, knowing he'd need its welcoming heat when he finally got the chance. He peeled off his coat and hung it over the stove, behind the chimney where it could steam itself dry, and followed it with the rest of his clothes which got draped wherever he could find space for them, as close to the heat as possible so they might dry out overnight. He'd literally been soaked through to the skin; his benefactor had also left a rather threadbare towel out for him, on the rail over the stove, and he wrapped himself in its dry warmth with a deep sigh of relief, rubbing himself down until his skin began to glow.

Clean dry vest, pants, shirt and trousers; fresh socks, a thick pullover and his spare boots; he slid back the hatch over the cabin doors and looked out to find that in typical fashion the evil weather had let up almost as soon as they'd stopped travelling. His sister waved from the other end of the boat, and he waved back:

'Pa an' Mam goin' ter the pub?' he called out; she nodded through the darkness:

'Yeah! You ready?'
'You bet Oi am!'

Five minutes later they pushed their way in through the door into the crowded front bar-room of the Greyhound. The other boaters within shuffled to make room for them, and the warmth of so many bodies backed up by a roaring fire in the grate almost had them gasping for breath after the bitter air outside. A raised hand waved to them over the heads of the crowd:

'Over 'ere Seph!'

They fought their way through; Joseph grabbed his brother's hand:

'Siah! Good ter see yeh...' he embraced his sister-in-law too: 'You too Joannie!'

'We got a load o' groceries fer Erdington, so Oi come this way ter see yeh.' Siah explained.

The families exchanged greetings all round, and Seph got drinks for his wife and children; settled together, squeezed in a corner of the room, Jacob spotted the newspaper under his aunt's arm:

'Wha's the news, Auntie Joan?' She chuckled:

'You missed it, Jake! I read it all out before, when there was still room to open the paper in here.'

'Oh!' She laughed at his disappointed expression:

'Oh Jake! As if I'd let you down! But there isn't much to tell, if it's the war your interested in. The fighting's all at a standstill, pretty well, with the winter weather. There's some going on near Verdun, the French against the Germans, but it ain't going anywhere if what the papers say is right. We're pushing the Turks back in Egypt so that's good, but the German U-boats are still sinking ships all over the place; the only good thing about that is that the Americans are getting more and more angry about it, so there's talk that they might join in one day, on our side.'

'Oh - right... Still ruddy complicated, ain't it?' Jake sounded mystified.

'We ran inter Kains at Christmas, in the Prince at Old Turn' Siah changed the subject.

'Oh ah?' Seph raised his eyebrows in query.

'Ah. They said ter pass on their 'ello an' good wishes ter you folks.'

'You give 'em the same from oos?'

'Oi did! Knew as yeh'd say that, Seph.' He looked at Ann: 'Oi got a message fer you an' all, girl. From 'Arold.' Her eyes lit up:

'From 'Arold?'

'Aye. Says as 'e's thinkin' 'bout yeh. 'E misses seein' yeh, if Oi'm any judge.' She glanced at her father, who just smiled at her:

'Oi misses seein' 'im an' all - would yeh tell 'im that when yeh sees 'im next?'

'Oi will that. Pity yeh ain't on the same trips as oos, yeh'd see 'im fer yerself then...'

'Oh - yeah...' She looked at her father again; he gave her a perplexed smile:

'Oi s'pose yeh're goin' ter get on at me ter go carryin' guns an' things too now, are yeh? Oi gets enough o' that from yer brother!'

'It's much better money, Seph; Joannie an' me's doin' really well out o' it, Oi've told yeh before' Siah reminded him.

'What is this, some kind o' conspiracy?' But Joseph was laughing: 'Furst you an' then Jake, an' now me daughter's on me case an' all! Well - is there still loads ter be 'ad, Siah?'

'Oh yeah, they're still lookin' fer more boats. D'yeh want me ter foind out fer yeh?' Seph stared at him, and then looked around at his two children:

'H'all roight! Foind out an' let me know, eh? Tell 'em as Oi moight be h'interested if there's steady work there.'

'Thank yeh Pa!' Annie flung her arms around his neck and kissed him on the cheek.

'Suit you an' all if we gets it, Jake?' Seph asked his son.

'S'roight Pa; be doin' better fer the war, eh?'

'Yeah, all roight! Yeh've made yer point!'

Chapter Eighteen

Harold Kain gazed around at the bright white countryside. A late cold snap had left a thin coating of snow across the fields, a light skim of ice on the water making a tinkling sound as the *Avon's* fore-end pushed along the channel broken by the passage of the *Tiber*, a hundred yards in front. It was a clear, sharp day after the snowfall of the previous night, the sky above a thin icy blue, a weak sun glancing across the fields of the canal summit as they headed away from the top of Long Buckby locks towards the deep darkness of Braunston Tunnel, a mile or more away. Ahead of him his father stood at the tiller of the *Tiber*; in the distance Libby's rump swayed gently as the mule plodded along, and between the boats Buddy moved in unconscious rhythm at the end of her own towline, drawing the deep-loaded *Avon* eighty feet behind her.

They'd stopped for the night below the locks, under the high embankment that carried the London & North Western Railway half a field away from the canal on its parallel course. They were running late on their usual weekly schedule; a jovial drink in the Spotted Cow, an earlyish night, and they'd started up the flight in the morning's darkness, delayed by the need to clear broken ice from behind the gates at each lock before they could run the boats in. They'd only cleared the top as the sun rose behind the hills to their right to light their progress amid the first stirrings of traffic on the Watling Street which crossed the water there. More delays awaited them, they knew - the chances were they'd have to wait a while for the steam-tug to take the boats through the tunnel while the girls took the mules over the top of the hill on the boat-horse road. And then there were the six downhill locks to Braunston village, although by then other boats would have broken and cleared the ice for them.

Beyond the junction with the canal to Leicester they passed under a succession of farm bridges; then a long gentle turn to the right as the ground began to rise around them. The flow of water from Daventry Reservoir pushed the boats away from the towpath, but first Alf and then his son easily compensated for it,

106

so familiar now with the road as to be barely aware of doing so. Both mules knew their way now too, and plodded along stoically with no need for encouragement; but then a horse appeared on the towpath in the distance, coming towards them. Harold saw his father bend to speak to his wife in the cabin below; moments later Mary appeared and took over the helm, swinging the stern of the boat in to the bank so that Alf could jump the gap and hurry ahead to catch up with Libby.

His own crew sat in front of the cabin, their backs to him, chattering as young girls will even if there is nothing to talk about.

'Suey! Emmie! One o' yeh get orf an' get ahold o' Buddy, there's boats comin'.' They looked around at him, and then lifted their heads to look forwards; Suey raised an arm in acknowledgement and stood up as he leant on the tiller to bring the stern in close to the towpath. She jumped, landing easily but grimacing back at him as mud splashed from under her boots before running forward and taking the mule by the bridle and slowing it to a standstill.

Convention dictates that canal boats pass on the right; for horse-boats that requires the 'outside' boat to come to a halt, its towline going slack to sink and rest on the bed of the canal while the 'inside' boat and its horse cross, passing over the fallen rope. Mary and Harold both steered away from the towpath on their left, the boats drifting to a stop opposite their respective mules, held still by his father and Suey. It was only as the *Avon* came to a halt that Harold looked up to recognise the approaching boat, its pony just passing Libby with a toss of its head, and a smile spread across his features. Another boat was following, two hundred yards behind the *Sarah Ann* - not unusual, the munitions boats often travelled together for mutual comfort, aware of the potential hazards of their cargo.

He watched the boat approach, and was puzzled momentarily to see a smaller head bob up over the cabin-top beside Siah Campling. The youngster waved furiously, and as they drew closer he recognised Johnnie; close enough for his voice to carry, he raised it and called out:

107

'Johnnie! Yeh back on the boats?' The figure nodded eagerly:

'Yeah! It's great ter be back! Oi'm 'elpin' Ooncle Siah fer now!'

'It's good ter see yeh! Yeh're better now?' Closer, and he let his voice fall. Johnnie nodded again:

'Yeah, mooch better thanks. An' Oi can read an' wroite! 'Ow 'bout that?' They were down to near-normal tones as the boats passed.

'Good fer you! Where's yer Mam an' Dad?' He turned to follow the conversation; Johnnie just gestured behind him, but Josiah chuckled:

'They's on the moonitions wi' oos now! Comin' be'ind.' Harold looked - his heart gave an involuntary leap as he saw that it was true, the other boat drawing closer moment by moment was the *Alice Rose!* He turned back:

'Tha's woonderful! See yeh soon?' Siah nodded:

'Aye - tek care lad!' Johnnie was waving furiously again as they drew apart; but Harold's thoughts were all for the other boat and its crew. Jacob was steering as the *Alice Rose* came closer; he raised a hand in greeting:

'Wotcher 'Arold! 'Ow yeh doin'?' And then there was another figure at his side, standing in the stern well, a shy smile on her face, and he found his throat tightening up so that he could barely speak. She waved, hesitantly, as if not sure of her reception, and he waved back; swallowing his nerves, he raised his voice again:

'Annie - it's so good ter see yeh...' Her smile grew wider:

'You too, 'Arold. 'Ow've yeh been?'

'Better now Oi've seen you' his answer slipped out before he could think about it, and he saw her blush at his words and avert her eyes. But then she looked up again, and her smile lit her brown eyes with a deep glow:

'We're on this trip now, 'Arold. Mebbe we'll see yeh sometoimes.'

'Oi 'opes so Annie!'   The boats were passing now, their voices lowered; the shy smile on her face had a hopeful look about it:

'Oi 'opes so too...'   Jake was taking it all in, a huge grin on his face:

'Tha's moy little sister yeh're chattin' oop, 'Arold Kain!' Harold found himself echoing the grin, knowing that the implied warning in the older boy's words wasn't meant:

'Oi knows that, Jacob Camplin'!'   Annie was laughing at their banter, and as the boats drew apart again Harold caught sight of her mother's face in the open cabin doors, a wide smile on her own face, and his heart lifted, knowing that that look meant his feelings for Annie were likely to be accepted by her parents.

The sudden snatch forward as Buddy took up the tow almost had him off-balance, so absorbed was he in his own thoughts. He grabbed the tiller, holding the stern of the boat in close so that Suey could jump back aboard; he blushed as she gave him a big happy grin over her shoulder and sat down. The two girls heads bent together, their chuckles coming back to him over the cabin-top, and he didn't need to be told what they were talking about...

Chapter Nineteen

The next week stayed cold, but the late-February temperatures were just enough to prevent the canals from freezing hard. Every morning would bring a light skim of ice which would crackle under the fore-end of the boats as they set out for their day's journey, but every day would bring enough warmth to melt it before midday, and it never got thick enough to jam the lock-gates or hold them up as they went about their business. An occasional shower of snow kept the fields under a blanket of white which would glisten as the sun struck across it, almost clearing under the day's thin warmth only to be re-established by a fresh fall overnight.

Monday February 26th, 1917: The two boats belonging to the Campling brothers were returning to Birmingham from that first trip together carrying rifles and bullets by the hundreds and thousands to Brentford for onward shipment to France where the troops were awaiting them in the trenches. Loaded with cases of tinned food for Birmingham, it suited them to run together; each crew knew the other so working together was second nature to them, and it meant that Johnnie could go to help his aunt and uncle while still travelling with his parents and siblings, something that was important to him after a year and a half away from them. Josiah knew the road, so the *Sarah Ann* led the way; the *Alice Rose* trailed two hundred yards behind, Molly getting used to following Socks along the towpath so that she could be left unattended for miles at a stretch.

Horses and mules are intelligent creatures, and most horse-boatmen relied on the idea of 'backering', leaving the horse to find its own way along the towpath; and most horses soon got to know a particular road, even learning exactly where to stop for each lock, so that a simple whistle or word served to control the progress of boat and crew. But on a new road, Ann had walked with Molly, stopping and starting her as they passed down the flight of six locks that descend to Braunston village; and now she stayed with the pony through the darkness as they passed the new pump-house and reservoirs that fed the short summit pound of the canal that they had left forty minutes before.

It was late and pitch dark, clouds building up overhead and threatening another overnight snowfall; the towpath under her feet was a soft mess of mud, churned up by boots and hooves since the morning's thaw, and she was praying that her uncle would soon call a halt. Up ahead, Socks was plodding easily along, Joan beside her, a hand on her bridle, and the pony knew that rest and a nice warm stable were imminent. Other boats were tying up for the night, and as they passed the entrance to the old canal arm that was home to the local depot of Fellows, Morton & Clayton Ltd with its cast-iron towpath bridge Joan drew her pony to a halt just beyond the toll-house. Josiah and Johnnie jumped off to tie the boat up; Annie let Molly slow to a stop behind Socks as her father brought the *Alice Rose* up against the side of the *Sarah Ann*. He and Jacob snatched the boats together, tying them securely; Annie took Socks' bridle from Joan and led both ponies away to the stables provided by the Grand Junction Canal Company beside the FMC dock.

On the boats everyone relaxed, getting washed and tidy for the short walk to the pub; a disappointed Johnnie was put to bed by his aunt:

'You're not eleven yet Johnnie, you're a growing lad and you need your sleep! We won't be long, I promise.' Tired after a long day ending with the lock-flights of Buckby and Braunston, heavy going even in good weather - not that he would have admitted it of course - he was soon sound asleep on the side-bed.

The ponies fed and watered, quickly brushed down, Ann made her way back to the boats to get clean and tidy herself. She was about to step over to the *Alice Rose* when she caught sight of a familiar pair of boats further along; her heart leapt and she quickly walked along to reassure herself of what she had suspected: *Yes!* Kains' boats! There was no light in the cabin portholes, but she knocked anyway; receiving no reply, she turned back with a hopeful smile on her face: *They'll be in the pub, fer sure!* She kept her news to herself, knowing that her

111

family would be pleased to see their old friends but looking forward to their surprise.

'We goin' ter the Castle or the Ship?' Jacob asked as they gathered on the towpath, wrapped in their heaviest coats. Both pubs were commonly used by the boaters - the Ship stood by the road, beyond the truncated arm which now served as Fellows's dock; the Castle was the more popular with passing boatmen as it was beside the canal a little further on where the road crossed the waterway. The brothers exchanged enquiring looks:

'Castle, Seph?'

'Suits me, Siah.' They set off, talking together about the day's trip, and everyone else tagged along behind. Annie was happy; somehow she felt that the Claytons family would be there rather than having gone around the dock to get to the Ship. And she was proved right; as they pushed into the smoky, crowded bar-room, a voice haled them from the far corner:

'Siah! Seph! Over 'ere!' They made their way apologetically through the busy room to join the Kains:

'Alf - Mary - good ter see yeh!' Greetings, handshakes and embraces were exchanged; Harold's eyes met Annie's, and they stood smiling at each other nervously for a moment:

''Ello 'Arold.'

''Ello Annie. 'Ow are yeh?'

'Oi'm foine, 'Arold; you?' They spoke quietly.

'Yeah, grand, thanks.' He reached out and took her hand: 'Yeh looks lovely ternoight...' She giggled:

'S'only me usual steppin'-out clothes!'

'Yeh still looks lovely ter me.' She held his eyes, her own reflecting the smile in them:

'Yeh're lookin' foine too, 'Arold.'

The older boatwomen had come together in a little group over their glasses of stout, Beth and Joan taking theirs as Siah passed them over; Mary had overheard the exchange between her son and Beth's daughter; she nudged the other woman and

112

inclined her head to draw her attention, and Beth replied with a broad grin:

'Them's gettin' on well, ain't they?'   She spoke barely above a whisper, and the other two women nodded conspiratorially:

'Reckon so, Beth! 'Ow old is yer Annie now?'

'Sixteen las' November.'

'Old enough to be courtin', eh?' Joan interjected.

'Oh aye! There's been boys sniffin' around fer a whoile, but she ain't wanted any o' them.' Her mother sounded proud.

'Waitin' fer ar 'Arold, d'yeh reckon?' Mary asked.

'Aye, could'a been.'

'Yeh don' moind? If 'e starts seein' 'er, Oi mean?'

'T'ain't oop ter me! But Oi don' reckon as Seph'll h'object, 'e loikes yer boy.'

'Suits oos too, Oi knows Alf's fond of 'er. Lovely girl, yer Annie.'

'Yeah, ain't she? 'E'd best be askin' Seph 'fore it goes on too long though, 'e knows 'ow it's done.'

'Oi'll mek sure as 'e does, don' woorry Beth.'

In their own little gaggle, their men had got to discussing the war; Siah and Seph were relatively up to date thanks to the Sunday paper Joan had bought the previous day in Leighton Buzzard:

'They reckon as the Germans are pullin' back Alf! 'Ad yeh 'eard?'

'That roight? D'yeh reckon as they're beat?'

'Dunno Alf. What they said in the paper didn' sound loike it; s'pose we'll 'ave ter see.'

'S'got ter be one oop fer oos though?'

'Guess so! An' we're doin' h'okay in Messo-somewhere too, beatin' the Turkish lot.' Alf laughed:

'Be h'all roight if Oi knew where the 'Ell that moight be!' The brothers joined in his laughter as Jake informed him:

113

'It's somewhere in the east, where it's 'ot an sandy! Oop by Palestine Oi think.' He sounded amused at his own ignorance: 'The h'important thing is we're winnin', eh?'

'S'roight' his uncle agreed: 'An' the h'Americans are gettin' more an' more angry wi' the Germans - what were it they said a week or two back, Seph?'

'They broke off relations wi' them. Diplomatic, loike - tha's what the papers said.'

'Wha's that mean?' They all chuckled again:

'Dunno Alf! Sounds koind'a serious though, don' it?'

'Means they ain't talkin' ter each other, loike. Koind'a loike when you an' Mam 'as a fallin' out!' Jake made them laugh out loud.

'Seems loike it's goin' ar way though, don' it?' Alf suggested; but Jake shook his head:

'Oi dunno, mister Kain. It all sounds good but... After all this toime...'

''Ow old are yeh now, Jake?' Alf asked.

'Seventeen.'

'Eighteen this year?'

'Ah - end o' June.'

''E's still 'ankerin' after goin' an' joinin' in' his father interjected: 'Be old enough then, 'e will.'

'Yeh don' want 'im ter, Seph?'

'No! There's too many o' them gettin' killed. But if they calls 'im oop, there ain't much Oi can do 'bout it, is there?'

In the corner, Harold had plucked up enough courage to slip his arm surreptitiously around Annie's waist; his heart had given a flutter when she raised no objection but settled comfortably into the crook of his shoulder. A head taller than her, he looked down into her big brown eyes:

'It's lovely ter see yeh agen, Annie.' He spoke softly so that no-one overheard. She smiled up at him:

'It's grand ter see you too, 'Arry.'

'Are yeh on this trip agen?'

.

'Aye - Pa's taken this on reg'lar. Moonitions ter Brentford, an' back wi' groceries fer Birnigum, tinned stuff mos'ly.'

'We're on the tar from Northampton, ter Springfield. H'every week. We'll be seein' more of yeh, then?' She wriggled in his arm again:

'Reckon so!' He echoed her grin:

'Tha's good!' He paused: 'We gets a trip in every week, loike Oi said. Pa usually stops 'ere on a Monday, then the Cape on Tuesday. The trip back's not so reg'lar, depends 'ow quick we gets empt at Springfield.'

'So we knows where ter foind yeh Mondays or Tuesdays, then?'

'S'roight!'

A little later, as both families strolled back to their boats for the night, they trailed along behind through the darkness, the towpath mud under their feet crunching softy as it began to freeze. Clouds rolled overhead, but only the very finest sparks of snow drifted in the air; parting at the Kains' boats, Beth and Mary glanced back, sharing a compassionate smile at the two youngsters following along, hand in hand, lost in their own world.

Chapter Twenty

6am in the morning; Suey and Emmie Kain were astonished when their big brother accompanied them to the stables for the mules. But they exchanged knowing looks when they found Annie and Johnnie Campling there before them, gearing up their ponies for the day's journey. They descended into giggles, much to Harold's annoyance, when he left them to deal with the harnesses and instead went to talk to Annie.

''Ello, Annie.' She'd heard them approach and looked around with a shy smile:

''Ello 'Arry.' He grinned:

'No-one calls me 'Arry! Only yer little brother.'

'Johnnie?'

'Ah!' She chuckled:

'Do yeh moind?' He shook his head:

'Oi'd loike it if yeh calls me that. Sounds - more friendly, loike.'

'Oi want ter be friendly wi' you, 'Arry.' The look in her eyes had his heart fluttering. He followed as she led Molly out into the morning where the faintest lightening of the sky was beginning to open the day; she paused, looking around; Johnnie pushed past, leading Socks by his bridle:

'Coom on Annie! We gotta get goin'.'

'In a minute, Johnnie.' She turned to Harold, gesturing at a boat which lay beside them in the arm: 'Them's steamers are they, 'Arry?' The boat in its smart black and white livery had an extraordinarily long cabin, and an odd rounded stern: 'Foonny shape, ain't they?'

'Yeah, mebbe. Don' 'alf go though!'

'Oi know! We 'ad one coom by oos th'other day, near washed oos oop on the bank. Ain't much room fer the load though, 'ave they?'

'Fellers's uses 'em fer h'urgent stuff what 'as ter be got there quick. An' they tows a butty along, mostly.' She'd picked up the tone of envy in his voice:

116

'Yeh fancies one, does yeh?' He looked down at her, smiling at the amusement in her voice:

'Not 'alf! I reckon's that's the future o' the cut. They got a few now wi' motors in an' all, 'ave yeh seen one o' them?' She shook her head, and he pointed across the dock: 'Over there look - tha's the *Linda,* see 'ow moch smaller the cabin is? Got a Bolinder h'engine, that 'as, joost as quick as a steamer but wi' more load space. Tha's got ter be the way it'll be in the future, eh?'

'Yes, 'Arry!' The sound of tolerant amusement in her voice had him grinning down at her; they laughed together at his enthusiasm: 'Oi gotta go, 'Arry.'

'Yeah - Oi'll be seein' yeh soon?'

'Oi 'opes so, 'Arry.' They stood looking into each other's eyes; Harold found himself stuck for parting words, but then Annie reached up and put her arm around his neck. Pulling him down, she kissed him quickly on the lips before letting him go and turning away, embarrassed at her own forwardness; hurrying away after her brother, she looked back with a smile and a wave. He waved back, still astonished but oh so happy at her parting gesture - until the giggles of his sisters brought him down to earth.

***

The first half of 1917 brought dramatic developments on the world's stage, news of which as ever spread through the boating community by word of mouth, like the ripples from a stone tossed into a pond. The political upheaval in Russia and the abdication of Tsar Nicholas II caused eyebrows to be raised even if it meant little to them in real terms; equally, British gains in Palestine and Mesopotamia were applauded with little genuine understanding of their significance. The announcement of America's declaration of war against Germany was greeted with rather more enthusiasm although the nuances of her declared status as an 'associate power' rather than a full ally of Britain was lost on the boatmen.

Victories at sea meant more to them and were greeted with joy, the Royal Navy gaining the upper hand in the North Sea and bombarding German bases in Zeebrugge and elsewhere; and the launch of British and French offensives on the western front similarly raised spirits only for them to turn to a sense of outrage when the news of mutinies among the French troops spread. And more outrage was stimulated in early June by bombing raids, German Gotha aircraft brazenly attacking London in broad daylight and causing many casualties as well as damage to buildings and property.

But through it all, Harold Kain's mood grew increasingly upbeat. He hadn't realised just how much he'd missed seeing Ann until their chance meeting and then that bitter cold night in Braunston where they'd quickly caught up on more than a year apart. Since then they'd seen each other quite frequently, usually passing by on the move and exchanging no more than a quick greeting; but even that limited contact served to lift his spirits every time. And four times (he could count and recall every minute of every occasion) the Campling convoy had managed to arrive at one of their own regular overnight stops, in Braunston or at The Cape in Warwick, and they'd had an evening together.

Only a part of their trips shared the same route - between Gayton Junction where his own boats would leave the Grand Junction Canal to get to Northampton, and Kingswood Junction where again they would turn off to take the easiest road to Oldbury and their destination. And while their trip would fit neatly into a weekly schedule, there and back, the Camplings' trips would take ten to twelve days from loading with arms in Digbeth to unloading in Brentford and then returning with foodstuffs or raw materials to various destinations around Birmingham. But quite often their northward trip would see them sharing the Kains' route into Birmingham, heading to unload at one of the City's central wharves; and that allowed added opportunities to meet.

118

Harold had turned seventeen in March, and he'd plucked up the courage one evening in the Cape of Good Hope to tackle Joseph, egged on by Ann:

'Mister Camplin'...'

'Yes, 'Arold?'

'Mister Camplin' - it's about Annie - well, 'bout me an' Annie. We're, well, quoite fond of each other...'

'Tell me soomat Oi 'adn't worked out fer meself, lad!' Harold blushed at his words although the grin on his face was encouraging:

'Er, yeah, well - would yeh moind if we kep' on seein' each other? Mebbe stepped out tergether, sometoimes?' Joseph laughed and clapped him on the back:

'If Oi was ter say no Oi'd never 'ear the last of it! If ar Annie's 'appy wi' yer coompany then that's h'okay wi' me, boy. But she's only sixteen, moind - no 'anky-panky, eh? An' if yeh oopsets moy girl yeh'll answer ter me *an'* 'er big brother, roight?'

So now he was 'officially' courting, and all was right with the world; or at least with his own little corner of it.

Not that courting was an easy state to be in, for the people of the boats. With such an itinerant lifestyle, just getting to see your intended could be a frustrating exercise - no simply walking along the street to call on them, taking them for a walk in the park or a trip to one of the new-fangled moving picture palaces. Harold's opportunities to see Ann came along no more frequently now than before; snatched conversations as the boats passed in opposite directions, the occasional fortunate arrival at the same overnight stop. But now, knowing that he would be welcomed by Ann's parents, he would set out to walk some miles along the towpath to meet them if there was a chance that they were tied up within reach of his own boats' stopping point, if they had crossed paths late in the day perhaps.

But maybe the old adage about absence was especially true for the boaters - his feelings for her remained as strong as ever despite their limited meetings, and he knew they were reciprocated in full measure, so that when they did meet their

119

time together was memorable. And sometimes they would take the opportunity to be alone together, escaping from they watchful eyes of their families - not that, given the mores of the time, that resulted in any ''anky-panky' as Joseph would have described it!

Thursday June 28th 1917 - a balmy summer evening, dusk barely gathering as the two Clayton boats traversed the two-mile pound above Bascote locks. Harold strode out along the towpath, following a few paces behind Buddy; he wasn't needed there, the mule knew her way so well by now she could have done the entire journey without human support. But it was such a beautiful evening, the air warm and still, the sun sinking behind him lighting the undulations left by mediaeval farming in the fields beyond the canal, that he'd waved Suey to go on without picking him up as they'd left the two-lock staircase that was the top of the flight of four. Now he was enjoying the exercise and the fresh air at the end of a long but satisfying day.

At seventeen, he was old enough now by the standards of their employer to be a captain in his own right, to take charge of the *Avon* independently of his father. But it suited them both to carry on as they were, running the two boats together, Alf the paid captain, his wife, son and younger daughters his crew, living on his income. Paid a set rate by the load, so much a ton, they couldn't have earned any more working separately, and with a regular trip that needed two boats the family could stay together - best for the girls while they were still young, to have their mam and pa around! But one day he'd have his own boat. With Annie? The idea set his heart racing, his spirit soaring...

He glanced back, and Emmie waved to him from her seat on the deck in front of the cabin. Looking forward again, his mother leant on the tiller of the *Tiber*, maybe fifty yards away from him; eighty feet in front of the boat, Libby's rump swayed, her tail flicking now and again, easily drawing the empty boat along at a fine pace. They'd had a good run, all the way from Warings Green, down Lapworth locks, down Hatton twenty-one, Cape two, across the Avon Valley and back uphill again:

Radford, Fosse three, Wood Lock, Welsh Road and then Bascote four. Deliciously tired, he was ready for the stop his father had suggested at the Two Boats at Long Itchington, just below the uphill run through Stockton locks.

Under the railway bridge - less than a mile to go. Over the small aqueduct; Bickley's Bridge, and next the road bridge loomed in sight. He saw his father step up onto the gunwale at the stern of his boat, clamber onto the cabin-top and walk forward, then down onto the long deck and up to the fore-end; peering ahead, he waved them through the bridge and jumped across onto the towpath with his fore-end mooring line below its arch, walking forward until he stopped Libby with a whistle, the boat coming to a halt just short of another already tied there, facing towards them. His mother stepped off with the stern line, and in moments the boat was secured to the rings set there for the purpose.

Alf beckoned his son on, waving for him to tie the *Avon* outside the *Tiber*. Under the bridge, and Harold drew Buddy to a halt next to Libby; Suey steered the boat neatly alongside and threw her own line to loop over the T-stud on the other stern. Emmie had run down to the fore-end and did the same there, drawing the two boats tightly together. Alf had walked up to his son; he nudged him on the arm and nodded to the boat they'd pulled up in front of. Harold looked, and a happy grin spread across his face making his father laugh:

'Thought yeh'd be 'appy ter see that, boy!' The boat was the *Alice Rose.*

Chapter Twenty-One

The boats moored, Suey and Emmie led the mules away to the pub's stables, giggling with each other when they saw the radiant look on Harold's face and noticed the reason for it. Johnnie Campling was playing just along the towpath with a couple of other boatee children; he spotted Harold and ran up as Alf disappeared into his cabin to wash and change his shirt:

''Allo 'Arry!' Harold ruffled the boy's hair:

''Allo Johnnie - all roight?'

'Oi'm foine, 'Arry!' The cheeky grin on his face matched the twinkle in his eyes: 'She's in the pub wi' Mam an' Pa an' Jake.'

''Oo'd that be then Johnnie?' The boy just laughed as he ran back to join his friends.

Impatient as he was to see her, Harold took the time to dive into his own cabin, strip off his dirty shirt and have a quick wash before slipping on his best one. Quickly combing his thick blond hair, he was out again and heading for the door of the pub; pushing his way in, he spotted the Camplings across the bar, through the smoky atmosphere, and waved a greeting. Joseph waved back, beckoning him to join them; Ann looked around and spotted him, and the shy smile he had come to adore lit her face as she came to meet him:

''Arry...' He slipped an arm around her waist and bent to give her a quick kiss:

''Ello Annie.' He led her back to her parents; Jacob grabbed his hand with a smile:

''Ow yeh doin' 'Arold?'

'We're foine Jake - Mister Camplin', Missus Camplin'. Pa an' Mam'll be along joost now.'

'Got soomat ter tell yeh, 'Arold.'

'Oh ah? Wha's that then Jake?'

'We'll 'old on 'til yer folks get in' Seph intervened: 'Will yeh 'ave a drink lad?'

'S'all roight Mister Camplin', Pa'll get 'em.' He glanced over his shoulder as the door opened: ''Ere they are now.'

Alf and Mary worked their way through the throng of boaters and local villagers to join them; cheerful greetings exchanged, Alf turned to the landlord and obtained drinks for his family. Everyone's attention back on the gathering, Harold asked his childhood friend:

'So wha's this news yeh got fer oos, Jake?' But before Jacob could tell them, his father spoke up:

'Been called oop, ain't 'e?' Eyes turned to Jake:

'That roight lad?' Alf asked; Mary's face expressed her concern, and Harold wasn't sure whether to congratulate his friend or commiserate with him:

'Wha' d'yeh think about that? Yeh still want ter go, Jake?'

'Oi ain't sure what ter make of it, 'Arold. They don' want me fer the h'army!' They were staring at him now, astonished:

'What, the Navy then?' Alf asked, but he shook his head. Again, Seph got in first:

'They wan' 'im ter go ter Dickinson's. Ter Croxley Mill.'

'Croxley?' Alf sounded incredulous, and Jake laughed:

'S'roight! Oi'm ter go an' work there.'

'Makin' paper?'

'Wha's that got ter do wi' the war, Jake?' Harold asked.

'We asked that, after Auntie Joannie read the letters fer oos. She got 'old o' someone there when we come by on ar way ter Loime'us. Seems they uses lots o' paper fer the big guns - they wraps the gunpowder in it, then it goes in be'oind the bullets. Navy uses a 'Ell of a lot, an' the big field guns fer the h'army.'

'Oh - roight.' Alf didn't sound convinced.

'Where's Joan an' Siah any'ow?' Mary asked.

'Ah! Got caught by the bloody Jerry h'aeroplanes didn' we? Oop by Moile End Lock, they coom over an' dropped bombs on oos! We got by, but Siah's boat got stoock when they 'it the towpath in front of 'im.'

'They're all roight?' Beth asked in horror.

'Yeah, they're h'okay, joost got covered in dust! They'll be 'long once they can get past.'

'Johnnie coom on wi' you, did 'e?'

'Ah. Misses 'is Mam's cookin', Oi reckon!' The laugh that followed had an air of relief about it.

'When yeh got ter go ter Croxley then, Jake?' Harold asked.

'S'posed ter be next Monday, but they said as it wouldn' matter if Oi were a day or two late. So's Oi can 'ave another few days wi' Mam an' Pa. We'll be back there fer Tuesday wi' any luck.'

'Oi'm not sorry 'e ain't goin' fer the h'army' Seph put in: 'There's too many lads as we knew ain't comin' 'ome as t'is - 'fraid they'd send 'im ter France once 'e got ter eighteen, Oi was.'

''Course yeh was, Seph.' Mary slipped her arm through his, her other through Beth's: ''E'll be safe enough makin' paper!' That had them all laughing. Alf was looking puzzled:

'Oi'd 'eard as yeh can get out o' the call-oop if yeh're a boatee, Seph?'

'Yeah!' Seph was scathing: 'If yeh can fill in all their bloody forms! What chance 'ave we got, eh?'

'Joannie could'a done that fer yeh, couldn' she?'

'Yeah - but they reckon as 'cause Oi got the missus an' Annie an' Johnnie Oi don' need 'im an' all. So it wouldn'a 'elped any'ow.'

'Loike yeh said, at least 'e'll be safe there Seph.'

'An' Oi'll be doin' a bit more ter 'elp, mebbe.' Jake sounded doubtful: 'Oi'd'a gone ter foight if they'd wanted me, but if they don'...' He shrugged.

'Yeh'll be doin' yer bit there in the fact'ry' Harold sought to reassure him.

'We're all doin' ar bloody bit! Where'd the bloody h'army be if we didn' get their guns an' stuff ter the docks, eh? An' bring all the groceries back fer the folks in Birnigum what works in the fact'ries?'

'Yeh're roight there Seph' Alf agreed: 'They'd be boogered without oos, wouldn' they?'

'Bloody roight!' Seph's flash of anger was beginning to cool; his wife took his arm:

'Everyone's doin' what they can, love. Whatever way they can, roight? Oos an' all.'

'Yeah, yeh're roight. Joost annoys me that some folks can' see that.'

''Ow's yer girls doin' lately?' Beth sought to change the subject.

'Jan an' Vera? They're foine - we goes that road sometoimes so's we can see 'em. Jan's goin' out wi' that manager fella we met! Noice boy; 'e's got a dodgy 'ip so the h'army don' want 'im, an' 'is job's h'important any'ow.'

'Tha's good Seph - she'll loikely stay on the bank then?'

He shrugged:

'Oi s'pose so - we'll 'ave ter see what 'appens, eh?'

'Nothin' mooch 'til this lot's over, Oi 'spect.' Mary added: 'Yeh remember young Albert Yorke?'

'Ah?'

''E got shot oop, real bad, lost a leg; 'e's in a sanitory 'ome in Birnigum. Ar Vera's goin' ter see 'im most days.'

'She were keen on 'im before, weren't she?'

'Reckon she still is!'

'Ah...'

'Wha's 'appenin' over there, d'yeh know?' Harold asked the gathering.

'First bunch o' Yanks 'ave gorn ter join in!' Jake informed him eagerly.

'That roight? Gotta be a big 'elp, ain't it?'

'Ain't that many of 'em though' Seph cautioned: 'They say as lots more'll be comin' soon, but it'll tek a whoile. An' in the meantoime the bloody French 'ave given oop!'

'What?' Alf was astounded, but Beth put them right, remonstrating with her husband:

'Tha's not strictly roight, Seph, now is it? What they're saying' she turned to Alf: 'is that some o' the French soldiers are refusin' ter foight, they've 'ad enough. An' mebbe yeh can' blame them! It moost be 'orrible fer the fellas what's stoock there in them trenches, oop ter their knees in mud all the toime.'

125

'Tha's all very well loove, but ar boys are still foighting! In *their* bloody country an' all!' Seph wasn't to be mollified.

'Yes, yeh're roight there - Oi ain't sayin' they're roight, joost that mebbe yeh can oonderstand 'ow they feel. There's a noo fella in charge o' them - what were 'is name?'

'Oh - er - Pet... Sommat. 'E's a top Froggie general, Joannie was tellin' oos.'

'Yeah; 'e'll sort 'em out Oi 'spect.'

'Oi bloody 'ope so! Whoy should we keep on foightin' fer 'em if they ain't?' Alf sounded almost as angry as Seph.

'We 'ad a big vict'ry a few weeks back, in Belgium.' Jake sought to change the mood.

'Oh ah?'

'S'roight - ar boys beat the Germans, blew lots of 'em oop an' took this h'important place off of 'em. Where were it Ma?'

'Place called Messines, Jake. Seems loike it's a big step for'ard fer ar fellas.'

'Tha's more loike it!' Alf's habitual grin was back.

'Serve 'em roight an' all!' Seph interjected: 'Been sendin' bloody h'aeroplanes over an droppin' bombs on Lunnon agen, ain't they?'

'That roight?'

'Yeah - in broad dayloight an' all! There was a lot o' folks 'urt an' killed a coupl'a weeks back.'

'So what're we doin' about it?' Alf asked; Seph shook his head:

'Not a lot, from the sound of it! Joannie said there's a lot o' argy-bargy 'bout it, 'ow we ortta be able ter stop 'em.'

Throughout this exchange, Harold and Annie had stood listening in, their arms around each other's waists; Annie nestled her head into his shoulder, raising her eyes to meet his:

'When'll you be eighteen, 'Arry?' she asked softly

'Nex' March. Not fer a whoile yet!' His reply was equally quiet.

'Tha's good. Oi don' want you goin' off foightin'. Nor even inter a fact'ry loike ar Jake. Not now Oi've found yeh agen...'

The families parted the next morning, heading their separate ways. Harold found himself getting quite emotional as he shook hands with Jacob, his arm around Annie's waist, a sense of emptiness gripping him as he said farewell to his childhood friend:

'Best o' luck Jake - yeh will coom back ter the cut when it's all over, won' yeh?'

''Course Oi will! Yeh can' see me stoock in a fact'ry fer the rest o' me loife can yeh?' Jake laughed.

'Aye, well - coom back safe, eh?'

'Loike yer Mam said, what can 'appen ter me, makin' paper?' Harold shrugged, grinning at his own silliness:

'Don' get wrapped oop in it, tha's all!'

They parted, laughing.

The horses harnessed, boats set off in opposite directions; Jake stood on the cases of tinned food in the hold of the *Alice Rose,* waving while Annie blew her beau a kiss from beside him. Harold was waving back from the tiller of the *Avon* until they were out of sight. His joy at seeing Annie, the knowledge he would see her again soon, was tempered by the thought that he might not see his friend again for a long time, maybe until the war finally ended - and who could tell how much longer that would take? For all the fighting it didn't seem that they were any nearer a conclusion.

For his part, Jacob was torn between anticipation and disappointment: The idea of work in a factory was something new and different, an experience to be taken even if he didn't see it as a change of career; but to leave the life he loved for what he saw as very much a subservient role in the war effort dampened his spirits. To go and fight would be different, something really worthwhile, but making paper? Even for use in shell-cases? He would have to do what was required of him, and he'd make the best job of it he could - but he was going to enjoy his last few days on the boats!

What he didn't know was that those few days would bring some high drama...

Chapter Twenty-Two

Josiah never did catch up with them on that trip - they were delayed for another day waiting for the debris from the German bombing raid to be cleared from the Regent's Canal. Unloaded at Crescent Wharf on the Ouzells Street Loop in Birmingham on the Saturday morning, Seph and his crew made their way around to the BSA factory in Digbeth in time to start loading a fresh consignment of rifles and ammunition later in the day. It was common practice for the ammunition boats to travel together for mutual support, uncomfortably aware of the hazardous nature of their cargo, so in the absence of the *Sarah Ann* they set off on Sunday afternoon in the company of two other boats, a pair belonging to Fellows, Morton & Clayton Ltd, also bound for Brentford. A good run, working on through a warm summer's evening saw them to the Cape of Good Hope in Warwick for their first night's stop.

Another good day, a clear road and long hours of daylight meant that their Monday took them all the way to the bottom of Buckby Locks and the Spotted Cow. Time for a quick ale, and the three crews retired for the night, Joseph and Jacob pausing for a last chat and a cigarette with the other captains while their womenfolk got the beds ready; Johnnie had passed up the opportunity to go to the pub with them, worn out after his long day, and was already sound asleep in the forecabin. Flicking their still-glowing stubs away, the men parted for the night, climbing down into their cabins.

'Pa!'
Joseph half-opened an eye in the darkness of the cross-bed.
'PA!'
He rolled onto his back and opened both eyes, his immediate reaction a flash of annoyance - it was anathema for anyone, even their own children, to intrude beyond the curtain that divided any narrowboat's cabin; Johnnie stood there in the dark, clad only in his underpants:
'Wha's oop?'

'Pa! Oi can smell soomat!'

He sat up now, alert, sniffing the air.

'Smoke, Pa! Oi can smell smoke!'

He drew a deep breath, and concern appeared in his eyes:

'Oi can smell it too Johnnie. Out o' me way, let's go see wha's afire.' He swung his feet to the floor, groping for his boots as his son stepped back to give him room. Annie was stirring on the side-bed:

'Wha's the trooble, Johnnie?'

'Smoke, Oi can smell smoke!' Her eyes grew wide, aware of the implications of fire on these boats, but she stayed where she was to allow her father to move around. His boots on his feet, Joseph squeezed past his son and climbed out of the cabin, looking around. Theirs was the first boat in the line of three, tied up to the towpath; Jacob, like himself wearing only his underclothes, was by the fore-end of the *Japan,* next boat behind them, leaning over its gunwale just below the cratch at the rear of its front deck. He looked up as his father appeared:

'Soomat's burnin' in 'ere, Pa!'

As he spoke, a flicker of flame appeared through a gap where the cloths met the deck-board.

'Oh 'Ell! Johnnie, run an' wake them insoide. Jake, dig out ar boocket from the fore-end, an' see if yeh can foind anythin' else we can use fer water.' The boys hurried to do as he said, and he grabbed the watercan from his own cabin roof. Taking careful aim, he poured its contents through the gap and saw the flames within die back. But moments later, as Jake ran back to him with the bucket, they flickered into life again.

He snatched the bucket and knelt on the towpath, leaning over to fill it from the canal; handing it to his son, he reached for the watercan and filled that too. Jacob pulled the cloths back unceremoniously, not worrying about undoing the strings holding them in place, and poured the bucketful in; he followed it with the water from the can as his father refilled the bucket. The boat's captain dashed up, roused by Johnnie's hammering on his cabinside:

'Oh Booger!' Quickly climbing onto his foredeck, he reached into the storage space beneath and retrieved another bucket, handing it to Joseph who immediately filled it from the canal: 'Johnnie - will yeh go an' tell moy missus ter get dressed an' out o' the cabin?'

'Roight, mister Beswick!' The boy ran back along the length of the boat; the three men formed a short bucket chain, Seph dipping the containers to fill them, Jake lifting them to Frank Beswick who poured the contents over the gunwale into his own cargo. But try as they might, their efforts were having scant effect, the flames only dying momentarily with each dousing before flaring up again. Johnnie was back, watching in horrified fascination; Seph glanced up at him:

'Run up an' see if yeh can raise the folks in the pub! Ask if they've got a 'osepipe, that way we can run it from the tap oop there.'

'Yes, Pa!' The boy ran off again. Elsie Beswick climbed out of her cabin in her working clothes looking shocked, and stood watching them; signs of life emanated from the Harrison's boat too, tied behind the *Japan,* alerted by the growing clamour outside, and moments later Joe Harrison was there to help, clad like the others only in his underpants and carrying another bucket.

Even with all four of them working as fast as they could, the fire was gaining ground, the highly inflammable material that comprised the cargo giving them little chance of stopping the growing conflagration; the flames were taking hold of the canvas cloths covering the cargo too now. Seph paused, mopping his brow:

'Where's that lad? We need ter get a 'ose on this if we can.' He bent to fill another bucket; Johnnie came dashing back:

'They're coomin' Pa! 'E's goin' ter get a 'ose outta their shed.'

'Well doon lad! Now stan' clear, eh?'

Bucket after bucket was thrown over the flames with little or no effect; glancing up, Seph saw the landlord emerge from the pub garden, a rolled-up hosepipe in his arms, and head for the

130

water-tap by the lockside. But at that moment too he heard a sudden loud crack from the depths of the fire, followed moments later by another; and then a succession of reports. His shoulders slumped, and he looked at the others:

'Bloody h'ammunition's goin' oop. We ain't goin' ter stop this.'

'What can we do, Pa?' Jake asked.

'Only one thing fer it.' Frank Beswick answered him: 'We gotta move the boat. If not the whole bloody lot'll go oop, yours an' all.'

'It's yer boat, Frank?' Beswick sighed:

'Aye. There ain't nothin' else fer it though, is there?' He jumped onto the foredeck and reached into the locker again, emerging with the towrope and handing it to Jake as he climbed off again. He reached out to take it back, but Jake was already stepping up onto the boat's gunwale, reaching for the top of the mast.

'Jake!' Johnnie yelled in horror - the fire had spread back now, and flames were leaping right below where his brother stood, licking up around his legs. He looked around with a grin as he dropped the loop of the rope over the towing looby atop the mast and jumped down to the towpath again:

'Don' joost stand there, go an' loose off the loines!' Johnnie grinned back at him and dashed to the stern of the boat; Frank was already untying the fore-end, pushing it out clear of the stern of the *Alice Rose*. Once the stern was untied as well, Johnnie gave it a good shove away from the bank and leapt on board, reversing the tiller in its socket in the rudder to steer around his own boat.

The men grabbed the uncoiled rope, led it alongside the *Alice Rose* and began to haul upon it, starting the burning boat moving; Jake climbed up to stand on his own boat's cabin and guide the line clear of the chimney and other obstructions that stood there. As the boat drifted past, he made his way along the top planks, keeping it from snagging anywhere on the mast or stands, jumping down onto the foredeck when he reached the front of the boat and so onto the bank again.

131

They hauled the doomed *Japan* several hundred yards along, past a lonely cottage that stood close to the canal, all the while the flames growing taller, the now-continuous rattle of explosions evidence of the boxes of ammunition burning, their contents going off in the intense heat. Fortunately for them, most of the bullets only drilled into the oak planks of the boat's hull; but some escaped to whizz off into the night, making them duck instinctively as they whistled over their heads. Well clear of any habitation, Johnnie steered the boat in to the bank; just as he jumped off a louder explosion made the burning boat shudder, an entire box of ammunition going off as the fire continued to spread. He ran back halfway towards the *Alice Rose* before turning around to watch; more bangs echoed into the night, most of the bullets contained by the hull but others escaping to fly off into the darkness above them. The three men stayed well beyond the *Japan,* aware of the danger of trying to get past it; Johnnie and the women stood with the pub landlord beside the *Alice Rose* watching in horror as the blaze took hold of the boat's wooden hull.

It took some hours for the fire to burn itself out, leaving the *Japan* no more than a hulk, its timbers burned away almost to the waterline. No-one dared to try to get close to the blaze; the rattle of exploding ammunition became a constant fusillade that didn't die down until the flames too began to subside, making them all remain in a low crouched stance while those bullets that escaped above the gunwales laid on an unwanted firework display. At last they could see that part of the cabin had survived, standing like a ruined castle at its stern; once the danger had passed, the men made their way back past it to join their families. Elsie fell into her husband's arms:

'Oh Frank! What'll we do?'

'We're h'okay, that's the most h'important thing, eh love? Gov'ment'll pay fer the boat, that was part o' the deal, roight? You're safe, tha's what matters.'

Everyone stood in a loose gaggle, Seph with Beth, Jake, Annie and Johnnie, and Joe Harrison with his wife and children, tired and shocked, the boatmen and Jake dirty and begrimed from their efforts to stop the blaze, the pub landlord still forlornly holding his hose in his hands. Light was breaking over the fields to the east; he looked around them all:

'You'd best all come up to the pub, you need a rest. And I guess a whiskey wouldn't hurt you fellows either. The missus'll be awake anyhow - I'll get her to light a fire and heat the water, you look like you could do with a bath!'

'That's really koind o' yeh Jack' Frank Beswick replied: 'Could yeh let the 'thorities know wha's 'appened an' all?'

'Josie will have called them already, I expect. Now come and take it easy for a while - you'd best all hang around until someone gets here anyway.'

***

It was midday before the surviving two boats were able to continue their journey; even then, they were only allowed to leave because of the vital nature of their cargo. A man from the government department which was now controlling the canal traffic had hurried to the scene, accompanied by an officer of the Grand Junction Canal Company; they'd taken a rather nervous look at the still-smouldering boat and then quizzed everyone about what had happened, to no real purpose:

'No oidea 'ow it started' Seph had told them, shaking his head: 'It were ar Johnnie as raised the h'alarm, 'e smelt the smoke an' gi' me a shout.'

'S'roight' the boy confirmed: 'Oi woke oop an' smelt soomat, so Oi got me Pa; we tried ter put it out...'

'You did very well, young man. And you jumped on board to steer the boat as they moved it, I understand?'

'Aye - well someone 'ad ter.' He glowed with pleased embarrassment as the man told him:

'That was very brave of you; your father must be very proud of you.'

'Oi am that!' Seph confirmed.

The inquisition over, they took their leave of the Beswicks, out of earshot of the officials:

'Yeh'll be h'okay, Frank?'

'Aye. We've got Elsie's old Mam in the cottage at Sutton's, we can stay there fer now whoile things get sorted out. Fellers's'll foind oos a new boat 'fore long, yeh'll see.'

'What about yer stuff?'

'Oh well' Frank shrugged: 'We'll get in there an' rescue anythin' we can. We'll manage!'

'Pa - Frank - we was stood roight there by yer fore-end las' noight' Jake spoke tentatively: 'Smokin' ar fags...'

'Aye - but we ain't tellin' *them* that, are we boy?'

Once again running late into the long summer evenings they made it to Croxley Green on the Wednesday night. Dickinson's management had arranged digs for Jake with one of their local families, much as the people at BSA had done for Jan and Vera Kain; on the Thursday morning he gathered his clothes and his few possessions and said an emotional farewell to his mother and brother. Seph and Annie walked with him to the factory and saw him into the hands of the shift manager, with apologies for his late arrival - a message about the fire and the delay to their trip had gone ahead of them thanks to the canal company.

Travelling on with the remaining FMC boat, and again running late each day, they caught up the half-day that had been lost to receive the praise of the management at Brentford's riverside dock.

Chapter Twenty-Three

Jonah Cherry came from a long line of canal workers. Never actually boatmen, his antecedents had included lock-keepers and lengthsmen - one of them, William, had achieved a level of fame as the man who had stanked off the canal when the Wolverton aqueduct collapsed back in 1808, thus saving both the surrounding countryside and the canal itself. Some of them, like Jonah, had become toll-clerks; often less than popular with the boaters because they took money from them for the 'privilege' of using the canals, toll-keepers were stationed at intervals along the network where they gauged the boats and charged the appropriate fee for onward passage.

Jonah, though, was not unpopular among the boatmen; a naturally cheery soul, he counted many of them among his friends. Charged with the important junction at Gayton where traffic from Northampton and the River Nene joined the Grand Junction Canal, he would see the same boats come by on a regular basis. And many of the boats that passed him now were the property of the bigger companies - Fellows, Morton & Clayton, Samuel Barlow, Thomas Clayton and others - whose passage he merely had to note as their tolls were paid on contract to the Grand Junction Canal Company.

A deep and dark December evening; snow had fallen intermittently throughout the day, if such a period of prevailing gloom deserved to be called day. Jonah stepped out of his door, pulling his heavy coat tighter around his shoulders, and walked briskly to the water's edge. He peered into a fresh flurry of snow, east towards the first bridge over the Northampton Arm, and then turned to walk to the junction and look north and south along the main line of the canal. With nothing in sight, he was only too happy to duck back indoors again, shaking the snow from his coat as he hung it behind the door.

A mile away, two deep-loaded tanker boats worked through the final locks of the Rothersthorpe flight. Harold huddled

135

behind the upturned collar of his coat as the snow, driven from behind them by the bitter easterly wind, whistled around his ears. The grey gloom of the day was almost gone, faded into the deeper darkness of dusk as he gave Buddy an encouraging slap on her rump and set off in her wake along the level pound that would take them to the junction. Behind him, his parents ran the *Tiber* into the top lock, themselves heaving a sigh of relief that the hard work of the arm with its rapid climb from the river valley was almost done. Nothing had been said, but the image of the welcoming warmth of the Navigation Inn by the junction was in every mind.

Jonah shrugged into his coat again as, peering out of the window, he saw the silhouette of the mule through the thinning snow across the junction. He stepped out again into the bitter weather, walking to the edge of the canal and cupping his hands to his mouth:

''Arold? That you lad?'

'Aye, it's oos mister Cherry! Pa's coomin' jus' now too.'

'Right - that's the *Avon* an' the *Tiber* then? Got yer loadin' tickets?'

'We 'ave, mister Cherry!'

'Right then! Yeh goin' on?'

'It's early ter be stoppin', Jonah!' Alf had caught up with his son now.

'Oh, *Pa!*' A voice sounded from the hatches of the *Avon;* twelve-year-old Emmie had had enough; Alf laughed:

'It's been a 'Ell of a day, eh? All roight, we'll tie 'round the corner.' It had been a long cold day and he was only too happy to give it a rest himself, but it wouldn't do to admit that to his children! And the aroma of the mutton stew on the *Tiber's* range was making his tummy rumble; Mary had put it on on the long pound below Wootton Lock, but there had been no chance to eat as they worked up from there, double-working every one of the remaining fourteen to pass both boats to the top.

They turned onto the main line, facing northwards for their destination, but a few yards clear of the turn they drew to a halt and tied the boats against the right-hand towpath. The two girls led the mules away, back and across the arm to the stables that stood beside it, where they soon got quite warm giving them a brisk rubbing-down in the stalls. On the boats, their mother served up hot platefuls of stew and dumplings to her men, keeping the pot on the range for herself and the girls when they returned.

Barely five o'clock, it was early for the boats to stop - normally, Alf would take them on, making for the Spotted Cow below Buckby locks three hours on. But even the hardened old boatman sometimes found the weather too much to cope with, and the seventeen locks of the Northampton Arm, worked in the slippery, dangerous conditions that day, the wind biting through the thickest of clothing, snow finding its way past collars and inside sleeves, had left him as eager to call a halt as his children. And beside the junction, next to the bridge which crossed the main line just there, stood the Navigation...

As Mary and her daughters sat down in the cabin of the *Tiber* for their meal, two other boats emerged from Blisworth Tunnel a mile and a half to the south. Conventional narrowboats, their laden holds enclosed under canvas cloths tied over the running gear, they drew in to the towpath behind the tug. In the darkness, almost as deep in the open as it had been in the depths of the tunnel under the heavy clouds obscuring the moon and stars, the tugmen cast off the tow and turned thankfully back to the tunnel and their waiting homes in Stoke Bruerne at its far end. Few boats were moving in the appalling weather, and they held an eager hope that they would not be needed again that day.

'Coom on Johnnie, toime ter get goin'.' Annie urged her brother into action, but the boy just looked up at her appealingly. Even in the shelter of the small stable he was shivering in his heavy coat; they'd deliberately walked briskly over the hill with the ponies to keep warm, but now they'd been waiting for a while for the boats to catch up with them. She put a sympathetic arm around him:

'Coom on, Oi 'spect we'll stop soon. Blizzerth, mebbe? Not far now, eh?' He nodded wearily, and they led the ponies out into the night. The snow had stopped falling now, and the deep cutting sheltered them from the wind; they took the towlines from the fore-decks of the boats and hooked them to the spreaders of the harnesses ready to set off again; Annie spoke to her father:

''Ow far we goin', Pa?' Seph looked at his brother:

'What d'yeh reckon, Siah?'

'We ortta get 'em ahead Seph, whoile we can. It's early yet, can' be past six o'clock.'

'We're all cold an' toired, Ooncle Siah?' Annie protested gently; he put a hand on her shoulder:

'Oi know - But we're all be'oind as 'tis. Bugbrooke? That ain't too far, eh?'

'H'okay, Ooncle Siah.' She turned to Johnnie, aware of his discomfort: 'You go an' sit in the warm, Johnnie, Oi'll go wi' Molly.' He nodded gratefully and headed for the stern of the *Alice Rose,* climbing aboard and ducking down into the cabin.

Taking the lead, she clucked the pony into motion; in such unpleasant conditions even the placid animal needed to be encouraged to keep moving. The line tightened, and the *Alice Rose* drew away from the bank; behind, Socks too leant into his harness, following his pal into the darkness and drawing the *Sarah Ann* along with him. Bugbrooke lay about halfway along the sixteen-mile pound to Buckby locks, maybe an hour and a half from where they were; despite her discomfort, Annie knew that even stopping there was a concession to the weather - her father and uncle would usually expect to make the bottom of the locks that night. She glanced back - Johnnie had vanished into the warmth of their cabin, the dark silhouette of her father stood hunched at the tiller, and not far behind she could see the even darker shape of Socks plodding stoically along the towpath, his white feet flickering in the night. She shrugged deeper into her coat, turning back to urge Molly into a quicker pace.

Around the S-bend of the cutting, the result of the tunnel being realigned halfway through its construction over a hundred

138

years before, and past the old mill by the turnpike bridge in Blisworth; around the back of the village, and under Candle Bridge; a long bend led them then through the fields, under a road bridge and then the railway, a train roaring and clattering over her head as they passed under the high arch. Another bend, under the branch line to Northampton, and they were approaching the junction where she led Molly over the turnover bridge to where the towpath continued on the left hand side of the canal, the lights in the toll-house drawing her envious gaze.

Once on the far towpath she drew the pony to a halt, waiting for the toll-keeper to appear. Behind her, Seph stepped off the boat as it drifted to a stop under the bridge. Socks had followed Molly over it, and stopped beside them, tossing his head disconsolately as if he too had had enough of the inclement weather; the *Sarah Ann* slid alongside the *Alice Rose,* Siah too bringing his boat to a halt to be gauged; Seph stepped across the boats to join his brother on the far side.

'Ruddy awful night eh, Siah? 'Ow are yeh, Seph?' Jonah strode across to them from the toll-house, gauging rod in hand. He quickly worked his way around the two boats, measuring the dry inches of hull above the waterline at each marked point on the gunwales, stepping on board one to check the other on the sides between them in the centre of the canal. Years of practice allowed him to hold the figures in his head until he returned to his office to write them down; moments later he was back to collect the few shillings due for their onward journey to the next toll-point. Duty done, he paused to chat with the two boatmen.

From where she stood opposite the junction itself, looking across the canal to where the arm disappeared away to her right, Annie caught sight of a pair of boats tied on the opposite towpath which led from the direction of Northampton, not far beyond. Something about them held her attention; strolling a little closer, she could make them out more clearly through the gloom - Clayton boats! The distinctive tank holds made them unmistakeable; and she knew which pair of Claytons worked this area! An opportunity to see her beau, to enjoy an evening in his company - she hurried back to the boat, calling across to her father:

'Pa! Pa! Them's Kain's boats, over there! Can we stop 'ere, please Pa?' Seph peered into the darkness ahead; two moored boats, across the way; Claytons, for sure:

'Oi guess we've all 'ad enough fer terday, eh? Oi'll see what Siah says.'

'Thank yeh Pa!' Seph turned to consult his brother, turning back with a grin on his face:

'Yeh can see yer feller, Annie! We're stoppin' 'ere fer the noight. We'll get cleaned oop an' go over the Navvie, h'okay?'

'H'okay Pa! Thank yeh!' Jonah grinned across at her:

'I'll see yeh all in there shortly then!'

She clicked her tongue to start Molly forward, drawing the boat from under the bridge, and stopped again far enough clear for her uncle's boat to tie behind them; both were quickly secured. She roused Johnnie from the cabin, and the two of them led the ponies to the stables; she was pleased to find the Kain's two mules there ahead of them, looking smart and contented in their stalls, and soon they had Molly and Socks looking equally relaxed and happy after a quick rub-down and plentiful hay. Then back to the boats; a quick wash and change into her best skirt and blouse, and the whole crew headed through the cold and the dark, over the junction bridge and to the welcoming lights of the Navigation Inn.

Chapter Twenty-Four

'It's a rum do, what's goin' on in Roossia.' Jonah Cherry was holding forth in the cosy bar room of the Navigation. Well read rather than well educated, he was nonetheless a man with an interest in - and views about - world politics.

'Dunno much 'bout it.' Alf Kain didn't sound particularly interested either, but Jonah went on anyway:

'Oh aye. First they kicked the Tsar out and their gov'ment took over - I mean, it'd be like Parlyment kickin' the King out, eh? Ruddy stupid! An' now this other lot 'ave kicked the gov'ment out! Call themselves Bolsheviks...'

'Wha's that mean, mister Cherry?' Harold wanted to know.

'Summat like the worker's party, they say. I mean, they're runnin' the country! Workers! Would you know 'ow ter run *this* country? I know I wouldn't 'ave the first idea!'

'Nor me Jonah' Alf agreed: 'Sounds pretty crazy, don't it?'

''Course it is! Won't work, trust me, you wait an' see! An' if they get their way we're goin' ter be in ruddy trouble, too.'

''Ow d'yeh mean, mister Cherry?' Harold was asking the questions still.

'Well, they've declared a cease-fire, right? Stopped fightin'; an' now the Jerries want ter make peace wi' them. If they do that, what Jerry wants is ter bring all 'is ruddy army that's been fightin' the Roossians back over 'ere an' set 'em ter fightin' our boys in France. That'll tip the ruddy balance in 'is favour, y'see?'

'Oh - roight. Oi thought we was doin' well, lately?'

'Aye, we were. Pushed 'em back quite a bit, captured a place called Passiondale - that's important 'cause it's 'igh ground, y'see. But if Jerry gets all them ruddy extra troops back, 'e could beat us back again, maybe push us right back.' He paused: 'Mind you, we're doin' well in Palestine. Knockin' the Turks fer six, good an' proper!'

'Oh, yeah... And we got the Yanks on ar soide now, ain't we?'

'S'roight boy, that's 'elpin' the more of 'em that get over 'ere - but there ain't enough of 'em yet, an' we could lose out agin all these extra Huns, see?'

'Meks yeh woonder 'ow much longer it'll all go on. Seems sometoimes loike it'll never end' Alf observed; Jonah nodded:

'Aye - we win a bit, they win a bit; they lose a bit, we lose a bit; don't seem ter be goin' nowhere, does it? Won't be won on the battlefield, you mark my words!' He gestured around them with his pipe-stem.

'What d'yeh mean, mister Cherry? 'Ow else can yeh win a flippin' war?'

'Ah! Well, yeh see, 'Arold, they reckon that Jerry's about runnin' out o' things at 'ome. Food, fuel all kind o' things. 'Cause the Royal ruddy Navy rules the seas! We get most of our stuff from abroad, right? America an' Canada especially, an' 'cause the Navy rules the roost out there our ships all get through - but Jerry can't get nothin', 'cause our glorious ruddy Navy's got ' im bottled up! They can stop any ships takin' stuff ter Germany, so we're slowly starvin' 'im out.'

'So yeh reckons 'e'll give oop in the end?'

'Reckon so, 'Arold. 'Ow long could you go on fightin' if yeh were always 'ungry, an' yeh didn't 'ave ammunition, nor petrol fer yer tanks?'

'Yeah, Oi see what yeh mean, mister Cherry. 'Ow much longer'll it take, d'yeh think?'

''Oo knows, lad! Not long, if what the papers say's right - next year, maybe?'

'Oi'll be eighteen soon...' They all looked around as the door opened, letting in a blast of cold air as well as the Campling families. Five more coats joined the pile in the corner of the room; Alf shook hands with Seph and Siah as the boatwomen embraced:

''Ow yeh doin' Beth? Joan?' Beth laughed:

'All roight now we're in the warm! Better still when moy man gets oos a stout each.' She looked pointedly at her husband.

'Johnnie on the boat?' Mary asked.

'Oh ah. Didn' fancy coomin' out in the cold agen!'

142

'We left Suey an' Emmie curled oop under their blankets too! Yeh 'eard from Jake lately?'

'Ah - we stopped in ter see 'im a coupl'a weeks back, an' 'e gets 'is mate from the digs ter wroite to oos now an' agen. Johnnie reads 'em out to oos - good thing 'e spent that toime on the bank wi' Granny! 'Ow's your Jan an' Vera gettin' on?' Mary laughed:

'Oi don' reckon we'll be seein' Jan back on the boats agen! She's talkin' 'bout marryin' 'er fella, that manager chap at the BSA. Vera's missin' the boats, though, she'll be back once the war's over, you wait an' see. She's still sweet on young Ably Yorke, the boy as got 'it by a shell in the trenches, reckons they could run a boat between 'em even if 'e as only got one leg.'

As Annie had followed her elders into the room, Harold had put down his glass and gone to meet her; helping her out of her coat, he returned her smile before taking her in his arms and giving her a quick kiss:

'Annie...' Her dark eyes echoed the sparkle in his blue ones:

''Arry...' He straightened up, this time kissing her on the forehead - his tacit teasing about the difference in their height made her giggle as it always did:

''Arold! Sometoimes Oi wonder whoy Oi loves yeh, the way yeh teases me.'

'Boot yeh do love me?' he asked in pretended fear, making her giggle again and give him a gentle slap on the cheek:

'Yeh knows Oi do, 'Arold Kain!' They were lost in their own world, stood in the corner of the bar room.

'Not as much as Oi loves you, Annie Camplin'.'

'Oh ah? Yeh ain't asked me ter marry yeh yet!' He leant back, holding her by the shoulders at arm's length, suddenly serious:

'Oi ain't goin ter neither, not as long as this bloody war's goin' on. Oi'll be eighteen nex' year - what if Oi gets called oop?'

'Yeh moight joost end oop in a fact'ry loike ar Jake - that wouldn' be so bad, would it?'

143

'Ah - but Oi moight get sent off ter foight. What then? S'pose Oi got 'urt? Or...' She put her hand over his mouth to stop him saying it:

'Oh, 'Arry...'

Joan had been aware of the trend of their conversation; now she interjected:

'How d'you feel about it, Harold? Would you want to go if they do call you up?' He turned to her, thoughtfully:

'If Oi'm honest, no, missus Camplin'. Oi s'pose Oi ortta, ter do me duty fer England an' all that - but what we do wi' the boats is h'important too, ain't it?'

'Yes it is Harold! *We're* keeping the army supplied, carrying arms to the docks, and the tar *you* carry is turned into all sorts of important products, lubricating oils for the guns and machines and things, so you're quite right. There's just you and the two girls on your boat, isn't there?'

'S'roight.'

'And they're only what? Fourteen...'

'An' twelve.'

'Too young to be in charge on their own! Working the boats is what they call a reserved occupation, Harold, important for the war effort, so you don't have to go.'

'No - Oi remember Jake sayin' 'bout that. But 'e still 'ad ter go?'

'Yes - because Seph had Beth, and Ann and Johnnie as well, on the boat. There's only the three of you! And two of them under age. There's forms to fill in...'

'Oi can' do that, though!'

'You can if I help you, Harold. Next time you get to Oldbury, ask the company for the forms - if they haven't got them they'll get them for you. And then we'll fill them in together. All right?'

'All roight! Thank yeh, missus Camplin'!' He turned and gave her a hug, kissing her on the cheek.

'Get away, you silly boy!' She pushed him away with a grin, only to be grabbed into a hug by her niece:

'Thank yeh Auntie Joan!'

144

Chapter Twenty-Five

And Auntie Joan was as good as her word. At the end of that trip, when they'd unloaded at the Springfield Works in Oldbury, Alf Kain took his boats for a brief stop on the Thomas Clayton yard a hundred yards along the Birmingham Canal. While he collected a new towrope to replace one that already had a number of splices along its length and was beginning to fray again, threatening to let them down, Harold picked up the forms he would need to fill in to apply for reserved status. The clerk in the office offered to help him fill them in, but:

'S'okay mate - Annie's Auntie Joan's goin' ter 'elp me do it. Pa wants ter be away as quick as we can now.'

'Okay 'Arold - drop 'em back in 'ere an' we'll send 'em in for yeh. 'Ow are things wi' you an' Annie?' Harold grinned cheerfully:

'Great! Once this bloody war's over Oi'm goin' ter ask 'er Pa if Oi can marry 'er.'

'Good fer you, 'Arold! I 'ope it all works out fer yeh!'

Their opportunity to fill in his forms came a few weeks later, towards the end of January, when chance brought the crews together in the New Inn, by the top of Long Buckby locks. Joan and Harold commandeered a small table in one corner of the lounge bar, a room normally avoided by the boaters; Ann stood looking over Harold's shoulder, her hand caressing the back of his neck and serving to distract him from the job at hand until he took it in his own, kissed it and gave it firmly back to her. Johnnie sat with them at the table, eager to show off his own skill at reading and writing; Joan entrusted him with the pencil, telling him what to write and watching his careful, neat printing as he took it down in the appropriate spaces on the papers.

Thence, Harold kept the forms safely away in the cabin of the *Avon* until their next arrival at Springfield; with no need to take the boats to the Clayton yard, he walked there while his father supervised the unloading and handed the papers back to the man in the office. And a couple of trips later:

''Arold - can yeh go an' see Bert 'Arris in the Clayton's office? 'E's got summat for yeh.' The message came via the foreman on the Springfield dock. Again, while Alf looked after the emptying of the boats, he walked across to the yard and into the office:

'Yeh got summat fer me, Bert?' The man grinned at him, turning to pick up an envelope from the pigeon-holes behind him:

'There yeh go, 'Arold! I reckon that's yer exemption - yeh can't get away from the cut, lad!' Harold grinned back:

'No more would Oi want ter, Bert! 'Ere, read it out fer me will yeh?' He handed the envelope back, and Harris slit it open, took out the letter within and glanced down it:

'Yeah, 'ere yeh go 'Arold - "exempt from conscription due to his reserved occupation as working boatman..." Like I said, yeh can't get away from us boy!'

'Yeah! That's grand, thanks Bert!' He almost snatched the letter back, turning away with a last 'See yeh nex' toime Bert!' and running back to the boats to pass on the news.

The swell of enthusiasm that had greeted the declaration of war in 1914 had amounted to a tidal wave, much of Britain's youth clamouring to join the army or the navy, eager for what they saw as the adventure of fighting for their country. The expectation had been for a swiftly-concluded conflict, a brief opportunity for glory and a rapid return to their homes - "it'll all be over by Christmas". But three and a half years of stalemate had seen that enthusiasm wither and die; even though British triumphs in the Middle East and the Royal Navy's successes in bottling-up the perhaps inappropriately named German High Seas Fleet in the Baltic Sea were trumpeted in the newspapers, stories and photographs of the trenches of Flanders had shaken the resolve of even the most hardened patriots. Many were coming to see the fighting on the Western Front as a futile, wasteful exercise, its progress measured in mere yards of

146

territory gained or lost, its cost counted in hundreds of thousands of young lives, destroyed by life-changing injuries or lost altogether. And there seemed to be little hope of any conclusion...

The next time that chance brought the Campling and Kain families together for an overnight stop came towards the end of February; Alf had decided to divert their trip along the 'middle road', staying on the Warwick & Birmingham Canal to its junction at Digbeth rather than following their usual route up the Stratford-on-Avon cut to Kings Norton in order to see his two elder daughters; Emily had run to the BSA factory as they passed in the afternoon, to let Janet and Vera know that their folks would be in the Prince of Wales that evening. And Joseph Campling, running empty across Birmingham to reload with munitions, hadn't taken much persuasion to stop for the night when Ann had spotted the *Avon* and the *Tiber* tied at Old Turn Junction.

It was an evening of joy for all - Harold brandishing the letter which exempted him from the call-up only to have Johnnie Campling grab it and show it off, reading it out to anyone who would listen to him; and Janet Kain had brought her young man with her. She'd prompted him with the way 'things' were done on the boats; he went up to Alf by the bar:

'Mister Kain? May I talk to you for a moment?'

'Aye - what is it, lad?'

'Well, mister Kain - I'd like to... I mean, would you allow me to ask Janet if she'll marry me?' Alf took the young man's hand with a wide grin:

'She's old enough ter make oop 'er own moind, boy. But you'll 'ave moy blessin' nonetheless, an' 'er Mam's Oi've no doubt.'

'Oh Pa! Thank yeh...' Janet threw her arms around his neck before turning to her mother: 'Mam...' Mary returned her embrace with a chuckle:

'If yeh're 'appy wi' this feller, Jan, that's all we want fer yeh.' She looked up at the tall young man: 'What do we call yeh? She ain't never told oos yer name!'

'It's Gerald, missus Kain, Gerald Grant. I used to shorten it to Gerry, but that's a bit awkward these days!' They all laughed as he went on: 'I'm Jan's shift manager at the BSA.' He drew Janet into his arms and gave her a kiss as Alf admonished him with a smile:

'You joost be sure an' look after ar girl then, Gerald!'

'Oh I will, mister Kain, don't worry!'

Harold had stood by, listening to this conversation, his arm around Ann's waist; she looked up into his eyes:

''Arry - you ain't goin' ter get called oop now, are yeh?' He gave her a smile, knowing that she was referring to his refusal to marry her while that threat had hung over him:

'Annie... Yeh're only seventeen yet. Oi do love yeh, yeh knows that, but yer Pa ain't goin' ter gi' yeh to me 'til we're a bit older, now is 'e?' He hesitated: 'An' Oi still ain't sure as we should any'ow, whoile this bloody war's still goin' on. They moight yet change their moind 'bout me, if it keeps goin' an' the girls get older.' He felt her shoulders slump:

'Oh 'Arry - Oi s'pose yeh're roight...' Touched by her disappointment, he squeezed her waist in his arm:

'Tell yeh what - the day they stop the foightin' Oi'll ask yer Pa if Oi can marry yeh, 'ow's that?'

'Oh 'Arry...' The look in her eyes had his heart aflutter.

***

The spring of 1918 saw Jonah Cherry's dire prediction coming true: With the political turmoil in Russia effectively ending her involvement in the war, the Bolshevik government had finally signed an imposed peace with Germany. And, knowing that the imminent arrival of tens of thousands of American troops could spell a final defeat on the Western Front, German General Erich Ludendorff began to transfer seventy divisions from the east to bolster his forces with the intention of delivering a rapid knock-out blow of his own. With a clear and he hoped decisive numerical advantage, he launched an offensive on March 21st, and by the time Harold had celebrated his eighteenth birthday, he had pushed the front line forward towards Amiens and Compiegne, close enough to Paris to begin bombarding the French capital with a number of eight-inch long-range guns.

But the British army, having fallen back some forty miles, finally dug its heels in as reinforcements were rushed up, and the French stood their ground in defence of Paris with typical Gallic tenacity. By early April Ludendorff was forced to accept that his decisive victory was beyond reach, and to resort to a series of smaller offensives aimed at gaining ground in a more piecemeal manner which would continue into May.

Chapter Twenty-Six

A bright cold April evening, and Johnnie Camping ran through the backstreets of Croxley Green. At 47 Alexandra Road, he stepped up to knock on the door:

''Ello missus Green, is Jake in?' The middle-aged lady who had opened the door to him smiled at the eager boy:

'He is that, Johnnie - I'll call him for you, shall I?'

'Yes please missus Green - we're tied by the mill an' Mam an' Pa want ter see 'im.'

Their return trip from Brentford, deep-loaded with tinned food for delivery to Birmingham's Crescent Wharf, had brought them to the vicinity of Common Moor Lock in the early evening, and Joseph had decided that the opportunity to see his eldest son outweighed the boater's usual instinct to cover as much ground in the day as they could. As they worked the two boats through the lock he'd suggested an early stop to his brother, and Josiah had readily agreed; they'd tied on the towpath and Ann and Johnnie had quickly taken the ponies to the stables attached to Dickinson's paper mill on the offside of the canal. And then, needing no urging, Johnnie had been despatched to rouse his older brother from his lodgings.

Ten minutes later the two of them were back; Ann grabbed her big brother into an embrace as he dropped the bag he was carrying and tousled her thick brown hair:

'Annie! 'Ow are yeh gal?'

'Oi'm foine Jake - it's grand ter see yeh!' She released him, for him to give his mother a big hug:

'Mam - yeh're lookin' well.'

'We're all h'okay, Jake - yeh're lookin' good an' all! Loife on the bank suits yeh, eh?' He shook his head:

'It's all roight, but Oi'll be glad ter get back ter the boats when this's all over!'

'An' we'll be glad ter 'ave yeh back, boy.' Joseph took his son's hand as his mother let go of him. Over his shoulder, Jake grinned at his aunt and uncle:

'It's great ter see yeh too, Auntie Joan, Ooncle Siah! Yeh're h'okay?'

'We're doin' foine, lad' Siah replied. Joan reached over to kiss his cheek:

'I'll put the kettle on, shall I?' A chorus of assent had her smiling as she ducked down into the cabin of the *Sarah Ann*.

A hubbub of voices erupted as they all began to bombard him with the news of the canals so that he raised his hands to slow them down. When he asked, Annie confirmed that she was still seeing Harold Kain, and her shy smile at the mention of his name had Jake laughing as he put two and two together:

'Gettin' serious, is it?' She nodded, blushing pink, as her mother joined in his laughter:

'Oi reckon as we'll 'ave yer sister married off 'fore too long!'

'*Ma!*'

'Well, tell me Oi'm wrong Annie?'

'Oh - well...' And they were all laughing again.

'Oi'm twelve now, Jake! Me birthday t'other day, it were!' Jacob turned to his little brother:

'Aye, Oi know, Johnnie.' He bent to retrieve his bag and delved into it: 'Joost as well Oi remembered ter get yeh a present then, eh?' The boys eyes grew wide as he took the wrapped parcel and tore it open:

'Oh wow! Thank yeh Jake!' He'd revealed a tin-plate model of a tank and was gazing at it raptly.

'That was koind o' yeh, Jake' his mother said: 'Moost 'ave been expensive?' He shrugged:

'Not too mooch. They pays me pretty well 'ere, an' any'ow 'e's me little brother, aint' 'e?'

Joan reappeared with handfuls of steaming mugs and passed them around, and the family relaxed as the dusk gathered around them. But through all the joy and frivolity, Joseph had detected something in his son's manner:

'Summat's troublin' yeh, Jake? What is it, boy?' Jacob sighed, as they all fell silent to hear his reply:

'Yeah - Oi was workin' oop ter tellin' yeh. Oi ain't stayin' 'ere mooch longer, they're sendin' me fer h'army trainin'.' The silence stretched out for a moment:

'They're sendin' yeh ter join the h'army?' Beth asked for confirmation, and he nodded:

'S'roight. In a coupl'a weeks toime. Wi' the way it's goin', the Jerries pushin' oos back, they want all the men they can get. Oi got a letter t'other day, an' missus Green read it out fer me. She's been teachin' me a bit o' readin' an' that, in the h'evenin's, but Oi ain't that good at it yet.'

'Oh Jake...' Beth sounded distressed, and her husband put his arm around her:

'T'ain't that bad Ma, 'e'll be h'okay, you wait an' see.' But the lines on his weather-beaten face told of his own fears even though Jake supported his words:

'That's right Ma, Oi'll be joost foine, don' you worry 'bout me eh?'

'Oi thought as there were lots o' Yanks comin' over now ter join in fer oos?' Siah queried; Jake nodded:

'Aye there are, but the Jerries are pushin' real 'ard an' they're 'fraid it won' be enough. There's a few other fellas from 'ere goin' an' all.'

**

Spring slowly turned into summer; continuing German offensives gained ground in a rather piecemeal manner, one thrust crossing the Aisne River, but the influence of the increasing numbers of American troops was beginning to tell. With their fresh strength bolstering the French and British lines as well as mounting counter-attacks of their own, Ludendorff was finding it harder and harder to make any progress, and indeed was beginning to be beaten back in some areas. Another major offensive in early June ended in abject failure, leaving the German commander-in-chief increasingly desperate...

And the other major partner in the Central Powers, Austria-Hungary, was suffering her own troubles. With the supporting

German divisions withdrawn to the Western Front, her war with Italy was under similar strain; an attempted offensive here too ended in failure in mid-June.

On England's canals, life and work went on much the same as ever. Under direct government control, much of the narrowboat fleet, company-owned boats and number ones alike, were continually employed on carrying in support of the war effort - the Kains, taking their gas-tar residues to be distilled into products like lubricating oils and soaps; the Camplings, keeping the allied armies supplied with guns and ammunition, and the factory workers of the midlands with food - even troops were often taken by canal from their training camps to the docks to be sent overseas to the fighting.

The boating community was as ever kept abreast of the war's progress by word of mouth, from wharf-hands and pub landlords as well as those among them who could read and write, and the apparent reversals suffered by the hated Hun were greeted with glee. And Joseph Campling was following his eldest son's progress with a mixture of pride and trepidation; Jacob had asked one of his mess-mates to write letters for him, and the weekly missive, passed on by the people in the Grand Junction Canal offices at Brentford, became a highlight of the family's life.

In early July they got a surprise, but one that eased their worries:

Mam, Pop, how are you all? I'm okay, almost finished my basic training now, and guess what? They're sending me to a place called Bovingdon, to learn how to drive a tank! I'm looking forward to that, it sounds like fun even if some of the other fellows say that they're horrible things to be in, hot and noisy and uncomfortable. It'll take a few weeks, and then I'll be going over to France to join in.

Don't worry about me - it's got to be safer in one of those things than running around with a rifle getting shot at, right? And they're saying that with more and more Yankee troops

153

arriving we're going to stop the Jerries once and for all, before too long. Won't that be good, eh?

Give my love to Annie and Johnnie; say hello to the Kains and all the other folks for me? Tell Harold I'm waiting for him to propose to our Annie! And maybe I'll be able to get home on leave for Jan's wedding - I'll try anyway.

Take care of yourselves; your loving son, Jake.

And in mid-August they received the first letter from their son in an official-looking envelope with a British Forces postmark from 'somewhere in France', taken down by his tank captain and duly censored, telling them that Private Jacob Campling was now a fully-trained driver with the Royal Tank Corps...

Chapter Twenty-Seven

The beginning of September saw the green of summer as ever slowly start to fade into the gold of autumn. But the changing colours weren't serving to lift Joseph Campling's mood - it was a chill and drizzly day, and as they'd taken the sharp turn under Kingswood Bridge, off of the Warwick & Birmingham Canal to join the Stratford cut, they'd been forced aside by a steamer emerging at speed in the opposite direction. Joseph had let his feelings be felt by the other captain in no uncertain manner, but that hadn't made the job of rearranging part of their cargo of boxes of tinned food - 'groceries' to the boatmen - that had been shifted by the collision with the bank any easier or quicker.

And now, as the evening drew in, they were nearing the top of the long flight of locks at Lapworth that would see them on the level run into Birmingham, around to Gas Street Basin where they were to unload. The delay would put them down the queue there, making them late for reloading at the BSA factory, hence Joseph's annoyance; his brother had come past them and gone on ahead, promising to wait for them at Digbeth before setting off southwards once more.

Four locks down from Lapworth Top, a quarter-mile pound separates the locks, taking a sharp turn under a bridge halfway along. And it is a truism of the canals that you will always meet another boat at the most difficult spot; Seph, at the tiller of the *Alice Rose,* gave a grunt of annoyance as he saw a mule appear under the bridge just as Molly, Johnnie at her heels, approached it. Johnnie brought the pony to a halt to allow the other boat to pass; Seph steered out to give it room. And then he recognised the girls following the mule, windlasses twirling in their hands.

They paused to exchange words with Johnnie, coming on with a last wave to the boy who kept Molly where she was. The mule tramped stolidly past him, past Beth and Annie who had stopped on the towpath just opposite him to let it by, and then girls were there, sharing cheerful hellos with his wife and daughter, calling across to him:

''Ello mister Camplin'! 'Arold's on the boat, an' Pa's comin' be'ind!'

'H'okay Suey, Emmie! See yeh 'nother day, eh?'

They walked on to the lock, and then the *Avon,* riding high and empty on its way back to Northampton, was passing him at the end of its towline, Harold leaning out of the stern well to talk to Annie before turning to greet him:

''Ow are yeh mister Camplin'?'

'H'okay, lad. You an' yer folks h'all right?'

'Aye we are, thanks. We'll stop at the Boot; 'ow 'bout you?' The Boot was the boater's pub, standing two-thirds of the way down the locks by another longer pound. But Joseph wasn't for stopping so soon, or walking back to a hostelry they'd already passed:

'We'll go on, Oi wants ter be out o' these'un's.' But then he relented, aware of the boy's desire to see his daughter: ''Ockley 'Eath, mebbe, ternoight.'

'Ah... Can Oi come an' see yeh later?'

'See ar Annie, yeh mean! If yeh don' moind the walk, boy.'

The boats were drawing apart now; Harold turned to share a parting wave with Annie, and then Alf Kain's mule was stomping towards him, the *Tiber* emerging through the bridge. More greetings were exchanged, and then they were on their way again, up through the last, more widely spaced locks of the Lapworth flight.

It was practically full dark when they reached the wharf and basin at Hockley Heath. Mindful of what he'd said to Harold, Seph suppressed his boater's instinct to 'get 'em ahead' and they tied just beyond the basin's entrance.

***

The mood in the public bar of the Wharf Tavern was upbeat. The admixture of boaters and working men from the small town were discussing the progress of the war; and now, at last, such discussions were carried on with a feeling of optimism. There was a sense that it was becoming a matter of time now until it could all be over - Germany's armies, having failed in their attempt to overwhelm the British and French, were falling back in the face of the growing weight of added American forces; falling back in some disarray, if the stories in the newspapers were to be believed.

And the news from elsewhere was promising: Italy was holding off another attack by the Austro-Hungarian army, and indeed pushing them back too; and the British victories in Palestine just kept on coming, the weary Ottoman Empire tottering under the onslaught.

Seph, Beth, Annie and Johnnie had joined the cheerful crowd after a quick wash and brush-up; three of them listening eagerly to the chatter, joining in, Johnnie telling anyone who would listen about their latest letter from Jake:

''E's drivin' one o' them tanks, an' 'e says as they're shovin' the Jerries back bit by bit, beatin' 'em all the way!'

Annie's attention to their talk was less intent, half her mind elsewhere, her eyes continually flicking to the door; and at last she was rewarded. The door opened to admit a weary-looking Harold, and she immediately eased through the crowd to meet him:

''Arry!'

''Ello Annie...' he bent to kiss her quickly: 'Said as Oi'd be along later, didn' Oi?'

'What are yeh 'avin', 'Arold?' Seph had spotted him too.

'Pint o' moild please, mister Camplin'!'

'Oh 'Arry - yeh walked all this way?'

'S'only 'bout three moile; an' it's worth it ter see yeh, Annie.'

'Oh 'Arry...' The look in her eyes had his heart fluttering again; Seph handed him a pint mug:

'There y'are lad, yeh'll be needin' that!' He took a long drink before bending again to kiss his girl on the forehead, making her giggle as that gesture always did. She reached up to run her fingers through his tousled blond hair as he bent lower to kiss her again, on the lips.

157

Johnnie was tugging at his arm, eager to get his attention:

''Arry! 'Arry...' He raised his head and looked down at the boy:

'What is it Johnnie? 'Ave yeh 'eard from Jake lately?' He guessed at the reason for the grin on his face, and Johnnie nodded:

'Ah, we 'ave!'

''Ow's 'e doin' then, yeh goin' ter tell me?'

''Course! 'E's doin' grand, droivin' 'is tank - 'e says as they're runnin' the Jerries out o' France altogether! We're goin' ter win, ain't we 'Arry?'

'Yeah, Oi reckons we moight, Johnnie.' Annie, her arm around his waist, gave him a squeeze:

'If we do, you remember what yeh said, 'Arold Kain!'

'Oi ain't gonna ferget, don' you worry, Annie Camplin'!'

***

And as the weeks rolled on, an Allied victory seemed to draw ever closer until the mood of euphoria began to match that which had greeted the outbreak of war four years earlier. Through September, in France and Belgium, the German forces withdrew to the fortified Hindenburg Line in an attempt to stem the Allied advance; in Palestine, the Turkish army under its German commanders was all but routed, collapsing under General Allenby's continuing offensives; and in the Balkan region the Bulgarian army was at the point of surrender to French General d'Esperey.

In early October, the Chancellor of Germany was ready to negotiate an armistice, but the Allied Powers were demanding the removal of the country's military leaders. Demoralised German troops continued to fall back in front of the British, French and American onslaught; the Italians continued to drive the Austro-Hungarian armies out of their country, and the Turkish government signed an armistice with Britain at the end of the month.

Morale in Germany had hit rock-bottom, fulfilling another of Jonah Cherry's predictions - ordered to sail for a last suicidal attack on the British fleet, the sailors of the German Navy mutinied, taking over not only their ships but the town of Kiel, their home base. And her armies too were ready to give up, soldiers surrendering in large numbers across the front lines in the west.

Austria-Hungary threw in the towel on November 3rd, agreeing an armistice with Italy; and at last, on the 7th, a delegation headed by German diplomat Matthias Erzberger began meetings with Marshal Foch in a railway carriage at Compiegne, north of Paris...

Chapter Twenty-Eight

Chance dictated that the *Alice Rose* and the *Sarah Ann* arrived, travelling together as ever, at Brentford's Durham Wharf late in the afternoon of Sunday, November 10th. Joining the queue to unload, Annie and Johnnie attended to the ponies, leaving them in the capacious stables; a riotous evening in the Five Bells followed, the knowledge rife now that the war was all but over, 'Kaiser Bill' abdicated and gone into exile. In the morning, as their turn came around to pole the boats against the wharfside and strip back the cloths and running gear, Johnnie made a bee-line for the canal company offices:

"'Ave yeh got any letters fer oos this toime, mister Rollin's?' The clerk chuckled:

'I have, young John! Two of 'em, this time - 'ere you go lad.'

'Thank yeh!' He grabbed the two envelopes, stuffing them into the pocket of his coat to be read later and running back to help with the unloading.

***

Running to their preferred schedule, the *Avon* and the *Tiber* had made it to Northampton on the Sunday ready to reload at the gas works. And in time for a quick trip into town, to the public baths, as was their habit. The chatter amongst the other customers was all of the end of the war, and Harold listened in with great interest, confirming with anyone who would listen to his questions that it was all but finished.

Walking back to the boats, he spoke to his father:

'D'yeh reckon what they're sayin's roight, Pa?' Alf clapped him heartily on the back:

'Seems so boy! Thank the Lord fer that, eh?'

'Ah... Pa - Oi promised as Oi'd propose ter Annie, when it was all over...' Alf stopped and turned to him:

'Then yeh'd best keep yer promise, 'Arold. I don' want no son o' moine breakin' 'is promises.'

160

'But - Oi don' know where they are, Pa?'

'Well, Oi reckon if we was ter ask the fellas at the Gas, mebbe they'd be able ter foind out fer oos, eh?'

***

Cases of rifles and boxes of ammunition stood stacked on the wharfside. The urgency that had seen previous loads hurried away to be sent on across the Channel was gone, fading under the mood of optimism that had everyone relaxed and laughing; and then, someone came running in from the nearby streets, waving a rushed-out special edition of the local newspaper, yelling at the top of his voice:

'They've give up! It's finished, it's all over!' Every head turned to the dishevelled fellow, a factory shift-worker, half-shaved in his vest, his braces dangling from his trouser waistband; he skidded to a stop, grinning all over his face:

'I thought yeh'd like ter know, see?' He burst out laughing, and all those around him joined in; Josiah grabbed his wife into an embrace, and they went dancing, cavorting around the dockside, and Joseph flung his arms around Beth, hugging and kissing her. Annie felt her heart soar: *'Arold 'ad better keep 'is word!* But he was who knew where? She'd see him soon... In the absence of her beau, she gave her little brother a long tight hug until he squirmed in her embrace and fought his way out.

No-one was in the mood to go on working; and there seemed no point anyway, if their cargoes were not going to be needed any more. Whatever the management thought, a general drift off into the town, towards the pubs that were unanimously unlocking their doors, soon became a tidal wave of celebrating men, their wives and children in tow, that crowded the bars and flooded the streets, singing and dancing through the afternoon and long into the evening. Annie, though quietly yearning for her Harold, let herself be swept along with them, laughing and singing with her arm around Johnnie's shoulders.

The chill grey day turned into a cold, dank evening - but nobody cared. The landlord of the Five Bells had long since run out of whisky, and he was eyeing his remaining stock of beers with some trepidation, aware that running out would not go down well with the riotous crowds surging in and out of his bar. And whether he would ever see many of his glasses again was debatable...

It was the middle of the evening when a tall blond-haired young man fought his way through the crowds along the High Street, intent on finding a certain one among the hundreds of revellers. It had taken him almost all day to get there, after his father had scraped together all the spare cash in his pockets to pay for trains and buses; but he'd made it at last. All he had to do now was find her:

'Annie! Annie, where are yeh?' His voice was all but drowned out in the noise, but he wasn't going to give up easily:

'Annie! I love yeh, Annie, where are yeh?'

Annie Campling looked around; dancing a jig with Johnnie and a group of other younger boaters, she thought she'd heard her name called. And again - and that voice..! She broke out of the dance, to stop, staring around:

''Arold?'

'Annie...'

There he was, incredibly, impossibly, before her.

'Oh, Annie...'

''Arry...'

They stared into each other's eyes, and she felt tears of joy trying to escape, saw the same glitter in his; and suddenly they were all alone, the crowds, the noise, the singing, the cheering, vanished as if it had never been, their eyes only for each other, the rest of the world banished. She flung herself into his arms, still not believing that he was really there:

'Oh 'Arry, Oi love yeh - yeh came an' found me!'

'O'course Oi did! Oi love yeh too, Annie...' He held her, stroking her thick dark hair, bending to give her a long, passionate kiss. Their lips parted, and she giggled breathlessly:

'Oh, 'Arry!' He laughed softly:

'So, Annie Camplin', are yeh goin' ter marry me then?' Her reply was just as quiet, her words warm and soft in his ears:

'O'course I am, 'Arry Kain.' He leant back, his arms still around her, gazing into her deep brown eyes:

'Oi love yeh, Annie.' She giggled again:

'Oi knows that, 'Arry! Not as much as Oi loves you though...' They kissed again; as she rose for breath, she reminded him:

'Yeh'll 'ave ter ask me Dad, 'Arry?'

'Oi will, don' you fear.' He looked around and laughed: 'If Oi can ever foind 'im in this lot!'

***

Johnnie had stood by, watching them, happy for his sister, delighting in her obvious joy and pleased that Harold would soon be his brother-in-law, part of his family. Harold had always been around, as long as he could remember, as Jake's friend before he was Annie's intended - Jake! He felt in his pocket, reminded of the two letters: *from Jake! Oi wonder if 'e knows it's finished?*

He looked around: Annie was in a world of her own, clinging to Harold, and his folks were nowhere to be seen. He shrugged his shoulders and wandered out of the crowd, down to the dockside where he sat on a bollard under a gas-lamp, taking the envelopes out of his pocket and gazing at them.

Usually, he would only open them to read them to his parents; but he didn't know where they might be. And it wouldn't hurt, would it? Just this once? He looked at them; one felt thicker than the other, and after a moment longer he tore that envelope open first, unfolding the two sheets of paper within. The heading looked official, but he ignored that and began to read:

Dear Mr and Mrs Campling,

I am writing to offer my very sincere condolences on the loss of your son. Jacob was a popular and well-regarded member of the regiment, and we will all miss him sadly...

Johnnie stared at the page, his eyes suddenly brimming: *No! This can't be right, it's a mistake!*

I know everyone under my command would join with me in offering you and your family their deepest sympathy, especially as his death comes so close to what we know will be an end to this conflict.

If it is any comfort to you, I can promise you that he didn't suffer. His tank was hit by an artillery-round from behind the German lines, and all of its crew were killed instantly. He will be buried here with the others, near Sedan; it is a very beautiful part of France despite the depredations of the war, close to the Belgian border...

Utter, incomprehending disbelief held Johnnie rigid, his mind frozen: *Jake! Oh Jake...*

Tears streaming unheeded down his face, he turned to the other envelope, hoping against hope that it would give the lie to that awful letter. He tore it open; inside was a printed telegraph form:

WE REGRET TO INFORM YOU THAT YOUR SON, PTE JACOB CAMPLING, WAS KILLED IN ACTION YESTERDAY, NOVEMBER 8TH. PLEASE ACCEPT OUR DEEPEST SYMPATHY FOR YOUR LOSS.

Time had stopped. Johnnie sat on his bollard, the letter and telegram crumpled in his hand, no longer hearing the sounds of revelry from the nearby streets, his world at an end, his mind numb:

Oh Jake... What am I going to do? You always led the way for me - now I won't be able to follow you any more... I love you, Jake - can you hear me? Please don't leave me...

***

A hand on his shoulder; he raised a tear-stained face to see Harold standing over him:

'We missed yeh... Johnnie? Wha's wrong?' He leapt to his feet and flung his arms around the tall young man who was going to marry his sister; Harold held him, ruffling the boy's thick curly hair, puzzled and worried by his distress. Annie, beside him, gently eased the crumpled paper out of Johnnie's hand; she peered at it, uncomprehending:

'Johnnie..?'

'Oh Annie... It's Jake...'

'What 'bout 'im, Johnnie?' She knew the truth before he could speak:

'Oh Jake! 'E's dead 'Arold, Annie - Jake's dead...'

'Oh Johnnie - oh *no*...' Harold stared into her eyes as they brimmed with tears, feeling his own eyes burning too as he gathered his girl into his arms. He held them close, feeling them both trembling as they wept for their brother, his own tears for his boyhood friend running down his cheeks...

The three of them stood like an island, a rock of grief set in the vast ocean of joy and celebration that continued to sweep over and around them as the rest of the world welcomed the long-awaited return of peace.

AFTERWORD:

Harold Kain married his Annie in June 1919. They worked for Thomas Clayton (Oldbury) Ltd, running their own horse-drawn boat, and for many years found themselves on the Oxford Gas Works traffic once again. Offered the chance of going on the better-paid fuel oil run from the Shell refinery at Stanlow on the Manchester Ship Canal to their depot at Langley Green, near Oldbury, soon after it began in 1924, Harold opted to go for it, and they remained on that traffic until he was killed in an accident on the ice-boat in the winter of 1938-9.

You will have seen from Wilfred Stevens' introduction that they had a son, Luke, in 1923; they were to have two more children, Alice, born in early 1927, and Rose, in 1930. After Harold's death, Annie continued on the boats, her employers accepting Luke as the nominal captain, turning a blind eye to the fact that he was under-age for that position. And in the late spring of 1939, they acquired another member of the crew in the form of a homeless half-caste boy called Jess Carter...*

And in August 1939, the 33-year-old Johnnie Campling volunteered for the Royal Navy. He served on various ships throughout the Second World War, emerging as a Chief Petty Officer. Choosing then to continue his naval career, he eventually retired as a Lieutenant-Commander after thirty years in the Senior Service, and later dedicated his memoirs to the memory of the older brother he had loved and lost so many years before.

*See 'Jess Carter and the Oil Boat'

If you have enjoyed this story, you can follow some tales of Annie Kain's later life with her children and their adopted crew-mate in Geoffrey Lewis' *Jess Carter* books.

And don't forget to check out his other writing about the days of our working canals; or take a look at his wider-ranging works of fiction, listed at the beginning of this book, by visiting www.sgmpublishing.co.uk